GUYAHOLIC

GUYAHOLIC

a story of

finding,

flirting,

forgetting . . .

and the boy

who changes

everything

CAROLYN MACKLER

CANDLEWICK PRESS
CAMBRIDGE, MASSACHUSETTS

Copyright © 2007 by Carolyn Mackler

First edition 2007

Library of Congress Cataloging-in-Publication Data is available.

Library of Congress Catalog Card Number pending

ISBN 978-0-7636-2537-5

2   4   6   8   10   9   7   5   3   1

Printed in the United States of America

This book was typeset in Sabon.

Candlewick Press
2067 Massachusetts Avenue
Cambridge, Massachusetts 02140

visit us at www.candlewick.com

CURR
PZ
7
.M2178
Gu
2007

To Juliet Eastland,

for saying just the right thing

at just the right time

Sam

It all started with the puck.

In March of my senior year, I went to a Brockport High School hockey game. I'm not a big sports girl, but I'd been hooking up with Amos Harrington since the past weekend and he played center and kept saying I should come cheer on the team.

I also went to the game because I didn't have work or rehearsal that afternoon. And my grandparents' annoying friends were visiting for the weekend, so I was steering clear of the house as much as possible. But most of all, Amos was my only current prospect. And more than anything, I hated being without a prospect.

Amos and I had fooled around three times in the past week. Once at a party, once at his house, and once in the auditorium after school. I'd never had a guy last longer than two weeks, and most of them didn't make it beyond a night. So with Amos's expiration date rapidly approaching, I needed to milk this for all it was worth or get out and scout new prospects.

I got to the rink late because my grandparents' friends cornered me in the kitchen. I had my headphones on, so I was hoping they'd get the hint. But Chuck hugged me, and Gwen, whose eyebrows were plucked into a permanent state of shock, gestured at my jeans and sleeveless red top and said, "You're leaving the house in *that*?"

I considered pretending I couldn't hear her, but my grandparents were hovering nearby, so I switched off my music. "It's not that cold out," I said. "Anyway, I'll be indoors the whole time."

"Won't you be at the ice rink?" my grandpa asked. "V, you just got over a sore throat, and you really should—"

"*Fine*," I said, gritting my teeth. "I'll take a sweater."

By the time I arrived at the game, the bleachers were jammed. I stood at the top, scanning the stands. Finally, I recognized some kids from *Chicago*, the play in which I'd just been cast as a lead. They were sitting down in the front row. I stripped off my sweater, stuffed it in my bag, and squeezed through the crowd until I reached Chastity and Trinity Morgenstern. They were identical twins and the biggest partiers I'd ever met, which was ironic given their names and those delicate crosses around their necks. The only way I could tell them apart was that Chastity's necklace was silver and Trinity's was gold. Also, at parties

Chastity tended to make out in public places while Trinity consumed massive amounts of alcohol and then conked out for the remainder of the night.

"Hey, V!" Trinity said. "I love your shirt."

"Where'd you get those boobs?" Chastity asked.

"Victoria's Secret," I said. "My latest addiction."

"Among others," Trinity said, laughing.

"You're one to talk," I murmured.

As Chastity cracked up, I scanned the ice for Amos or, more notably, his butt. But before I compose a novel about the hotness of Amos's hindquarters, I have to interject a quick word about my boobs. I'm the first to admit that I'm not endowed in the mammary department and had recently begun siphoning my Pizza Hut paychecks into expensive padded bras. But guys love cleavage and, well, I love guys.

The hockey game charged forward. I was partially chatting with the twins, partially watching Amos, and mostly exchanging glances with a guy to my left and a few rows up. As I was maneuvering down the bleachers, I saw him check me out. He was wearing a canary-yellow jacket with a ski-lift tag hanging off the zipper. He had a coating of stubble and he looked older, like he went to college.

I shook out my hair and looked back at Ski Lift Boy. He was saying something to his buddy, and then he glanced at me with that lusty gaze that guys save for video games, red meat, and cute girls.

I'm not saying I'm this gorgeous prom queen, but my skin is clear and my nose is okay and my honey-colored hair is long and everyone tells me I have a good body, though it doesn't help that I'm taller than most human beings, at least the ones in high school. I think the biggest thing going for me, though, is that if there's an attractive guy in my radius, I can work it hard and generally get him interested.

Ski Lift Boy raised his eyebrows as if to say, *Do I know you?* I smiled back, already envisioning how we could meet near the concession stand and exchange numbers and I'd go to his dorm tonight and he'd have a single room so we could—

"WATCH OUT!"

I whipped my head around in time to see the hockey puck hurtling toward me, but not in time enough to dodge it.

I heard the impact as it splintered my forehead. I felt intense pain. I sat still for a second, totally stunned, before wilting backward.

Someone shrieked, "Oh, my God! She's been hit!"

Someone else screamed, "Call 911!"

Someone else shouted, "Does anyone get cell-phone reception in here?"

My head landed in a lap. My eyes were closed, and there was blood leaking onto my hair. And the pain. *Oh, my God.* The pain.

The person with the lap pressed a sweatshirt against my forehead.

"I'm sure it looks worse than it is," he said.

I wondered how bad it looked.

"Is she dead?" I heard someone ask.

"The ambulance is here!" someone else announced.

"Should they bring in the stretcher, or can she walk out?"

I recognized the voice. It was that genius who'd just wondered whether I was dead.

"Real genius," the guy with the lap muttered.

If I weren't dealing with a major head injury, I would have cracked up. But it's hard to laugh when you're drenched with blood and possibly dead.

The guy with the lap kept pressing the sweatshirt to my head.

I remember smelling basil and garlic.

I remember thinking it smelled good.

I got eighteen stitches in my forehead. My grandparents made me wait in the emergency room until they located the best plastic surgeon west of Rochester. As my grandma called around, my grandpa held a leaky bag of ice on my head.

Once I was stitched together and scanned for internal bleeding, we drove home. I had a massive headache and an even more massive bandage on my forehead. That night my grandpa came into my room every hour and made me tell him how it was March sixth and my name is Vivienne Vail Valentine but everyone calls me V. By the fifth visit, I was so fed up I considered telling him I was Marie Antoinette, but I didn't feel like being rushed back to the emergency room in the middle of the night. Then again, I wouldn't have minded another ambulance ride with that hot paramedic who kept calling me Princess.

I stayed home from school on Monday. That afternoon Amos stopped by. Any other day I would have led him directly upstairs, but my throbbing forehead wasn't getting me in the mood. Not to mention I was wearing dingy sweats and couldn't take a shower until the stitches came out. I'd attempted to scrub the blood out of my hair, but I still felt completely gross.

"How're you feeling?" Amos asked as we sat on the couch.

"I guess I'll be okay."

"Are you going to have a scar?"

"The plastic surgeon said I'll have a thin line down my forehead. Nothing huge. She thinks it'll fade over time."

"When can you come back to school?"

"Probably by Wednesday."

Neither of us said anything. I was getting the sense that when Amos and I weren't groping each

Sam

other, we didn't have much in common. As Amos listed the injuries he'd sustained from a decade of ice hockey, my forehead hurt worse and worse until finally I told him I'd better go lie down.

Amos stood up to leave.

"Oh, hey," he said, hoisting his athletic bag onto his shoulder. "I brought you something."

He reached into the side pocket of his bag and handed me a hockey puck.

"Are you serious?" I turned it over in my hands. "Is this it?"

"Some kids tossed it onto the ice after you left in the ambulance. I grabbed it for you."

"Uh . . . thanks?"

"Anytime."

A few hours later, the doorbell rang. I was stretched on my bed, waiting for a phone call from my mom, Aimee. She was living in San Antonio, Texas, managing a restaurant and shacking up with this guy she called the Cowboy. My grandpa had left her a message the night before and told her about the accident. She'd e-mailed me in the morning and said she'd try me at five, New York time. It was currently six twenty, but I still hadn't heard from her.

The doorbell rang again.

That's when I remembered that my grandparents, after making me promise I'd take it easy, had gone out to dinner with their friends.

Sam

I twisted my hair into a ponytail and headed downstairs.

Sam was at the front door.

No one uses the front door in our house, but he didn't know that yet. And I didn't know his name was Sam yet.

When I opened the door and saw this tall guy with blond hair that flopped over puppy-brown eyes, I said, "Thanks, but I didn't order pizza. Hold on. You don't have a pizza. Are you doing a fund-raiser?"

He stared at the doorbell as if he were surprised he'd actually pushed it and it had actually rung and I'd actually appeared.

"Are you selling those coupon booklets?" I asked.

He was squinting, even though the sun had long since abandoned western New York.

"Don't tell me you're a Jehovah's Witness," I said.

He scuffed his sneakers against the bricks.

"Or maybe you're registering voters? I don't turn eighteen until September, so you'll have to check back then. Except I might be away at college, but I doubt I'll get in anywhere, so we can meet here in the fall if you want."

He continued studying the doorbell. I knew I was coming on strong, but I have a serious thing for puppy eyes. Plus, this guy was taller than me and built without being steroidal, lanky without being a beanpole.

"Final guess," I said, glancing at the checkered gift bag in his hand. "You've come to ask me out."

I detected a hint of a grin. Great lips, by the way.

"That's it, isn't it?" I asked. "You have a thing for girls with greasy hair and bandages taped across their foreheads."

Now I got a full smile. Dimples, too.

"Do you have a name?" I asked.

"Sam," he said. "Sam Almond."

Sam Almond. Did he have the world's best name or *what*?

"I'm V," I said.

"I know."

My heart jumped. "You know?"

"You go to my school. We're both seniors." Sam paused before adding, "And you fell onto me at the hockey game yesterday."

"Oh, my God!" I clapped my palm over my mouth. After I was hit by the puck, I didn't open my eyes until that hot paramedic hoisted my stretcher into the ambulance.

"*You're* the guy with the lap?" I asked.

Sam nodded.

"Do you find it bizarre that you've had intimate contact with my brain matter?"

"No big deal." Sam shrugged. "I was happy to help."

"So I was right . . . you like bandages and stuff."

"Don't forget the greasy hair."

When Sam smiled again, I felt a churning in my stomach, like I was watching characters kiss at the end of a movie. Even though you know they'll probably break up five minutes later, in that moment everything is bliss.

"Oh," Sam said. "I brought you something."

"Please tell me you're not giving me the bloody sweatshirt."

"What?"

Before I could explain about Amos and the hockey puck, he reached into the checkered bag and handed me a loaf of bread with dollops of green squished across the top. It was encased in Saran Wrap, but I could distinctly smell basil and garlic.

"It's pesto focaccia," Sam said. "Homemade."

"I love bread," I said.

"I love to bake," Sam said.

I tipped my head curiously. He smiled. I opened the door wider and gestured him inside.

1

I graduate from high school on a rainy Monday in late June. The ceremony is being held at the college rink, site of my notorious collision with the puck, except the ice is gone and the walls are decorated with CONGRADULATIONS! signs, courtesy of the Spirit Club.

I know I should be ecstatic, given the fact that before I moved to Brockport I'd attended seventeen different schools in nearly as many states and was such a slacker I had little chance of receiving a diploma, much less a cash award for my theater contributions, which I'm going to be getting as soon as the principal stops blabbering about how we're all carrying torches into the future and gets on with the ceremony.

But I'm so anxious, I'm not relishing in any of the accomplishment stuff. Basically, I'm obsessing about whether my mom will arrive in time to see me walk across the stage. My insides are clenched. I can barely breathe. And I'm on the verge of chewing off my nails, even though I got a manicure yesterday before heading to the mall to spend the remainder of my cash on a black dress and strappy sandals.

I haven't seen my mom since January of my junior year, when she sent me to live with my grandparents. In the ensuing eighteen months, she's promised to visit three different times, twice for opening nights of plays and once for my birthday. But something has always come up and she's canceled at the last minute, leaving me miserable, depressed, and continually surprised, as if somehow I thought that this time things would be different.

And yet this time, things *are* different. Aimee and I have been talking on the phone a lot recently, less parent to child and more person to person. She's even said some stuff about how since she was only nineteen when she had me and barely knew my father, she's obviously screwed up a lot, and while she can't change the past, she's hoping to make it up to me in the future. In fact, the other night on the phone, Aimee said, "I want to know what your life is like these days. My time in Brockport will be all about you."

I even told Sam that Aimee is coming, and that's big for me because I generally don't talk about my mom with anyone other than blood relatives.

Yes, crazy but true, Sam Almond is still in the picture. After he appeared at my front door with the focaccia, we started hanging out. And then we started hooking up. And then, once we hit that two-week mark, when I usually decide a guy is too clingy or a sloppy kisser or has an unforgivably pointy nose, Sam and I continued hooking up.

It's been over three months, and I still don't know what to call us. We exist in this blurry zone that's more than friends with benefits and less than going out. It's a definite source of tension because Sam wants us to be boyfriend and girlfriend, complete with prom and promises and pictures in each other's lockers. The problem is he doesn't understand what it was like to grow up with a mother who acquired a different "serious" guy every few months. He has no idea what it was like to wake up on a random Sunday morning and encounter a man pouring coffee in our kitchen, scratching his crotch, and then reaching out his hand to introduce himself as "your mom's new boyfriend." Naturally, whenever I hear the B-word, I want to get in my car, hit the gas, and never glance in the rearview mirror.

But I haven't ditched so far. I'm not sure why, except Sam's eyes do me in. Not to mention that he's really into cycling, so he has legs that could launch a thousand orgasms. And he's really nice and mellow, so nice and mellow in fact that mostly I feel undeserving of him. Which is another reason to flee. But then there are those homemade baked goods he's always tucking in my locker. And did I mention Sam is seriously smart? He's going to Berkeley in the fall and majoring in history and minoring in political science. And did I mention his abs? It's good Sam wears a shirt in public because if he didn't, I'd probably get arrested for public displays of fondling.

"In conclusion," the principal says, "I want every person in the graduating class to carry a torch out into the world and start a fire."

A few of the seniors chuckle. Someone throws a beach ball in the air.

The principal clears his throat. "Not arson, of course. Metaphorical fires. I want you all to go out into the world and start metaphorical fires."

Another beach ball pops into the air.

"Without further ado—" The principal mops his forehead with a handkerchief. "Will the A's and B's please line up to receive your diplomas?"

I shift in my seat. I can see Sam heading toward the center aisle. His hair is exploding from the perimeter of his cap like unkempt shrubbery. As he turns and waves at me, my stomach does a happy little somersault.

But then I scan the bleachers and feel awful all over again. My grandparents are sitting midway up, the empty spot they've saved for Aimee gaping like a lost tooth. My grandpa has his phone pressed hard against his ear. I begin gnawing at my French tips.

This is *not* the way it was supposed to be. Aimee was supposed to arrive yesterday afternoon on a four-twenty flight. I'd just gotten home from the mall and was eating leftover buffalo wings before leaving to pick her up at the airport when my phone rang. As I glanced at the incoming number, I got a sinking feeling inside.

"Hey," Aimee said. "Something's come up."

She went on to explain how she was still in San Antonio because the Cowboy had been in the emergency room all day and they thought it was appendicitis, but now they're saying it's a kidney stone, and she missed her flight and didn't have a chance to call until just now.

"I'm flying standby first thing tomorrow morning," Aimee added. "There's a layover in Houston, but I should land in Rochester by twelve forty-five. I'll rent a car at the airport and come straight to graduation."

"Rebecca Aiello . . ." the principal is saying. "Nicholas Allcott . . . Sam Almond."

When I hear Sam's name, I clap loudly and shout, "Wooo-hooo!"

Sam must have heard me because as soon as he's shaken hands with the superintendent, he finds me in the audience, smiles, and raises his diploma in the air.

When I don't think too hard about things, it's good between Sam and me.

Great, actually.

In so many ways, he brings out the best in me.

We'd only been hooking up a few weeks when I received five straight college rejections. Honestly, I wasn't shocked. My transcripts had improved in Brockport, but on the days I'd shown up at my four previous high schools, I was generally smoking weed, skipping class, or chasing some guy. If anyone lectured me about academics, I'd tell them exactly where they could put their number-two pencil.

But then after my royal flush of rejection letters, Boston University wait-listed me. That evening Sam helped me compose a response, thanking them for reconsidering me and explaining how I was born to a teenage mom and had moved all over the country. Sam encouraged me to tell them that since arriving in Brockport, I'd starred in two musicals and one summer production at the college, and if I was accepted, I was going to be all over the Stage Troupe, which is this student-run theater group at BU. It was weird writing this stuff, but Sam insisted I send out the letter. Three weeks later I got a call from an admissions officer inviting me into their freshman class.

As the S's and T's receive their diplomas, I glance into the bleachers again. Still no Aimee. At this point I've chewed off all my nails. I wish I had my phone because I'd send her a quick text message, but there are no pockets in my gown and I couldn't exactly carry it in my hand during the procession.

"Do you know what time it is?" I whisper to the guy on my left.

He pushes up his sleeve. "Two fifteen."

"Thanks," I say.

Aimee should be here by now. Even if her plane landed late, she'd still have had time to make the thirty-minute drive into Brockport.

16

The principal instructs the U's, V's, and W's to line up. I adjust my cap and take one more look into the stands. Aimee's seat is still empty. As I step onto the stage, receive my diploma, and shake the superintendent's hand, I'm doing everything I can to swallow back the tears.

On the way back to my seat, I pass Sam's row. I can feel him smiling at me, but I make a serious effort to stare straight ahead.

When I think too hard about things, it's difficult between Sam and me.

Awful, actually.

In so many ways, he brings out the worst in me.

We'll be having a perfectly fine evening, like he'll meet me at the end of my Pizza Hut shift and we'll be munching bread sticks in the parking lot and then, out of nowhere, he'll bring up the whole relationship thing. I'll tell him if he's looking for a girlfriend, he's come to the wrong place. He'll say that it's just about letting myself love. And when he uses *that* word, I'll storm away and he'll call my phone and I won't answer and he'll call again and I won't answer and, finally, around midnight I'll text him to apologize and we'll return to hanging out and having fun and carefully avoiding certain conversations.

Aimee doesn't arrive in time to see me receive the Barker Weill Drama Award, and she doesn't arrive in time for the cap tossing, and as we're all marching out, I finally have to accept the fact that she hasn't arrived in time for any part of the ceremony.

As all the graduates are reuniting with their families, I can't find my grandparents, which is unfortunate because in that brief second that I'm standing by myself, I'm assaulted by Sam's mom's camera.

"Great picture!" she squeals. "I'll definitely put this one in Sam's senior-year scrapbook."

There's something about Sam's mom that annoys the hell out of me. Partially, it's her soccer-mom bob and closet full of machine-washables, as if she's never accepted the fact that she no longer has toddlers smearing applesauce on her clothing. Also, she knows all of Sam's and his sister's friends and always tries to keep tabs on who is hooking up with whom, and why someone broke up and what the big fight was about.

"Where's your mother?" Sam's mom asks me. "I'm dying to meet her."

Damn it, Sam. I told him Aimee was coming, but I didn't expect him to blab it to the entire world. Just then Sam and his dad show up. I say hi to Sam's dad and shoot a look at Sam.

"What?" he asks.

Sam's mom is watching us, so I shrug dismissively.

"Is your mom around?" Sam asks.

I'm still glaring at him when my grandparents emerge from the crowd. I can tell by the smiles plastered on their faces that they're working overtime at plastering. They hug me tight and gush about the Barker Weill Drama Award and how I strode so confidently across the stage.

Once I wriggle free, my grandpa clears his throat. "We just stepped outside to call Aimee. . . ."

"V's mother?" Sam's mom asks. "Where is she?"

"Something came up with her boyfriend," my grandma says. "He went back to the hospital in the middle of the night. It sounds like the kidney stone was causing a lot of pain and—"

"A kidney stone!" Sam's mom gasps. "How awful. That's supposed to be the worst."

"Aimee's still in San Antonio?" I whisper to my grandma.

"I'm so sorry," she says quietly.

For this horribly long moment, everyone stares at me. My cheeks are searing and my throat is tight, and even though I'm surrounded by the celebratory buzzing of graduates, the only thing I can hear is a voice in my head saying, *I can't believe you thought that this time things would be different.*

2

Sam walks me to my car. The plan is that I'm meeting my grandparents at the Red Bird, then heading over to the Almonds' for a barbecue, then going to a party with Sam and his sister, Rachel, and maybe one of her friends.

As Sam and I head out of the rink, we dodge hordes of graduates posing for pictures with their families. Neither of us comment as we pass three sets of mothers and daughters pressing their cheeks together, but by the fourth Sam says, "I didn't know your mom had a boyfriend."

"Yeah."

Sam is watching me, so I fixate my attention on my gown swishing around my calves, my fingers gripping my diploma, my new sandals rubbing the skin off my toes.

"How long have they been together?"

"I'm not sure." I pause. "Maybe since January?"

Sam doesn't say anything, but I can tell by the way he's edging closer that he wants to take my hand. I've always drawn the line on that. Kissing in public is one thing. It means you're hot for each other. But hand-holding is in another league. It means couple. It means commitment. It means I'd better fill up my tank because I'm going to drive a hundred miles in the opposite direction.

"What's his name?" Sam asks.

Why can't he quit it with the questions? Does he want me to admit I haven't memorized the names of all of Aimee's boyfriends? She only calls this one the Cowboy. Besides, there have been so many over the years that at some point I stopped wasting the brain cells.

After a moment I say, "I haven't met him, so . . ."

Sam gestures toward the rink. "Are you upset?"

"Not really."

"You're not upset your mom didn't make it to graduation?"

I sigh heavily and flip my hair over my shoulders. "Can we not talk about this anymore?"

As Sam and I walk through the heavy glass doors, he says, "I just wanted to make sure you're okay."

"Yeah," I snap. "No big deal."

Sam and I head across the parking lot. It's still drizzling out, and I can't help thinking that there's something about drizzle that makes me incredibly sad. It's so quiet you hardly know it's there until you realize your clothes are wet and you've been getting rained on all along. Also, the earthy odors are so strong—steamy pavement and mowed grass and wilted dandelions. I'm not sure why those smells are heartbreaking, but they just are.

Sam and I arrive at my car. It's a used black Volkswagen that my grandparents helped me buy last fall. I had to be at graduation early, so I drove myself over here, pried my key loose from the chain, and, for lack of a more modest crevice, slipped it into my bra.

"What you just said about it not being a big deal," Sam says. "You haven't seen your mom since she moved to Costa Rica, right? How long ago was that?"

My hands are trembling. I'm having a hard time fitting the key into the lock.

"I think it's more of a big deal than you're letting on," Sam says. "I think you should call your mom and tell her you're upset."

"*Sam.*" I clench my teeth. "I *seriously* don't want to talk about this."

I open the car door, lean in, and toss my diploma onto the passenger seat. As I do, I spot my phone resting in the drink holder. I quickly check for messages from Aimee. *Nothing.*

I don't exactly want Sam to know I was checking, so I drop my phone onto the seat, take a few shallow breaths, and trace my fingers over Demon Puck. That's what Sam always calls it. Basically, a few weeks after Amos brought me that hockey puck, I painted a smiley face on it and superglued it to my dashboard. Sam immediately dubbed it

Demon Puck because wherever you're sitting in the car, its eyes are always following you.

When I emerge from the car, Sam has his hands clasped behind his neck and he's looking up at the overcast sky. He's frowning and the rain is wetting his cheeks. I lean against the hood, and he positions himself across from me. I think he's about to kiss me, but instead he studies my face, like he's searching for answers. I don't happen to have any, so I stare back at him. He reaches over to touch the scar on my forehead, which is still purplish and a little tender, but then pauses and lowers his hand.

I glance down at his sneakers, my sandals, the oil shimmering in the puddles. I think about how much I want him to leave me alone right now, stop making me feel bad I'm not whatever perfect girlfriend he wants me to be.

"I guess I'll see you at your barbecue," I say.

"Or maybe we should meet in St. Louis?" he asks, grinning.

I have to smile. That's this dumb joke we have, but even so, it does the trick. We lean in for a kiss and it's soft and warm, and I instantly take back everything I thought about wanting him to leave me alone. Now I'm wishing we could pull apart our slippery blue gowns, press our bodies together, and ultimately end up somewhere horizontal. Preferably a bed, but I'd settle for a backseat.

I can tell Sam feels it, too. He wraps his arms around me, and we stay like that for a while, hugging and kissing and getting drizzled on. Then I hop into my car before either of us can do anything to screw it up.

Sam has no idea what he's saying when he tells me I should call my mom and let her have it. Granted, I've never given him much on Aimee, only that we ping-ponged from coast to coast until she sent me to live with my grandparents because she was moving to Costa Rica.

But I've never told him what happened in Seattle or Phoenix or Philadelphia or Burlington or even Eugene. And I definitely haven't told him about San Diego, which is where I lived before Brockport, because that would require talking about Michael and, so far, I haven't told anyone about Michael.

Michael was Aimee's boyfriend in San Diego. I know I said most of her boyfriends were nameless crotch-scratchers, but Michael was different. We'd only been living in San Diego for three weeks when they started dating. Usually, when Aimee landed a new guy, I wouldn't meet him until that morning-after moment in the kitchen or, worse, the day we showed up at his house with a U-Haul. But before Michael even visited our apartment, he insisted on getting together with me in a neutral spot. I remember it perfectly because some kids from school had finally asked me to hang out, but no, Aimee insisted on dragging me to some beach to meet some guy and walk some beagle.

My first impression of Michael was "Huh?" I know it

sounds shallow, but according to the laws of the dating universe, Aimee and Michael were a total mismatch. It's hard to rate my mom's attractiveness except to say that she's tall and skinny and has long, blond hair and people are always telling her she could be a model. Michael was short and bald with a honker nose. Plus, his dog's name was Mama, which made me wonder about his lingering parental issues.

But Michael turned out to be hilarious. He was a sit-com writer who did stand-up comedy on the side. Plus, he actually took the time to get to know me. All through June and July, if Aimee was working a double shift, he'd take me out to dinner or we'd bring Mama to the beach and he'd ask me about my life or what I thought of various jokes, and he'd actually listen if I told him something sounded dumb. Plus, he couldn't go ten minutes without a Starbucks, so he and I bonded over our mutual caffeine addictions.

In early August Aimee said we were moving into Michael's house. Michael let me pick a color for the guest room, and he and I spent a weekend chugging iced lattes and rolling on the paint. All through that fall, we watched the same shows and ranked the taco shops in the neighbor-hood and took Mama to the beach. Sometimes Aimee would joke that she was the third wheel, but mostly we were all having a good time together.

Around Thanksgiving Aimee stayed out late two nights in a row. Through December she got calls on her cell phone and dashed into the backyard to answer them. I sensed something was up, but I kept hoping if I didn't say anything, it would go away.

Right after New Year's, Michael flew to Vancouver for three weeks to film a made-for-TV movie. The day after he left, Aimee came home with a sunburn when she was supposedly at work all afternoon. As soon as I saw that, I cornered her in the kitchen and told her she'd better not hurt Michael. She acted all innocent, but the following week, she confessed to me that she'd fallen for a twenty-two-year-old surfer she met on Black's Beach. I started yelling and saying how I had no respect for her and she was a horrible person and I couldn't believe she cheated on Michael like that.

The next morning Aimee told me that she and the surfer were moving to Costa Rica and I was being sent to live with my grandparents. I never even got to say good-bye to Michael because, nine days later, Aimee put me on a plane to Brockport. After that I didn't hear from her for almost a month. And here it is, a year and a half later, and she still hasn't shown up.

When I arrive at the Red Bird, the hostess chirps, "Valentine, party of three that used to be party of four?"

I grunt and she leads me to my grandparents' table. As soon as I sit down, they're both suspiciously upbeat. They pour me a glass of iced tea and tell me how they've ordered an assortment of my favorite baked goods and they're so proud of me and I looked so beautiful in that cap and gown, and they're buttering me up so much I'm counting the seconds until they begin fishing for my innermost feelings.

I've just bit into a mixed-berry scone when my grandpa runs his hands through his gray hair and says, "How are you holding up?"

My grandma sighs heavily, all concerned and sympathetic.

It's lucky my mouth is stuffed because I have the entire chew and swallow to formulate a response other than: *How the FUCK do you think I'm holding up? I haven't seen my mom in eighteen months, and she canceled on me yet again because some random guy has a kidney stone and it's suddenly more important than her own daughter?*

Instead, I just shrug.

"You're really okay, honey?" my grandma says as she reaches over and clasps my hands.

"I know how much you were looking forward to seeing Aimee," my grandpa adds.

I wriggle my fingers loose and attempt to swallow back the lump in my throat. Seriously, what do they want me to say? Do they want me to tell them how, in the past few months, I've been having a hard time remembering what my mom looks like? It's little things you can't see in a picture, like how one of her eyelids droops when she's tired or that her elbows are so damn bony. Do I tell them I couldn't fall asleep last night because I kept envisioning how my mom would hug me close and then, still holding my hands, step back and say how great I looked, so beautiful, so grown-up?

My grandparents are still waiting for me to participate in their group-therapy session when my phone rings. I grab it off the table and quickly say, "Hello?"

"Hey . . . it's Chastity."

"Hey, Chas . . . what's up?"

"Trinity and I wanted to make sure you're coming to the party. It's going to be huge. This guy's parents are in England and basically don't care what he does while they're gone."

I assure Chastity that I'll be there. I can hear Trinity squealing in the background, and I'm about to ask whether I can crash their pre-party, but my grandparents are staring at me, so I tell Chastity I'll see her later and then hang up.

3

I totally don't want to go to Sam's barbecue.

That's what I'm thinking as I drive through town and turn into Sweden Village. The rain has stopped and the air is mild, but I still feel like crap. I'm just not in the mood for fielding all those "where are you going to college next year" questions, as if anyone actually cares because all they want to blabber about is where they went to college and where their kids went to college and where their kids' neighbor's dog went to college.

Honestly, all I want to do at this point is chill out, get a little tipsy. Okay, I'll be honest. More than tipsy. After the day I've had, I'm ready to get wasted.

But Chastity said the party isn't starting until nine or ten. It's not like I can spend the next four hours hanging out with my grandparents or cruising aimlessly around

Brockport, so I head down Hollybrook Lane, park on the curb in front of Sam's house, and slide on some lip gloss.

As I'm cutting through the side yard, I pause for a moment. Maybe I should head back to my car, call Sam, tell him I'll meet him at the party later. I'm just not in the right head space for this. But then I remember my lack of viable options, so I smack my lips together and continue into Sam's backyard.

I spot Sam right away. He and his sister are over by the laptop. They've set it up on a card table at the edge of the yard, under a flowering white tree. Rachel is angrily gesticulating, and as I get closer, I realize they're arguing about whose playlist to do next.

"V!" Rachel shrieks, waving me over. "Will you please tell Sam that he listens to fifty-year-old-dad music?"

"You listen to fifty-year-old-dad music," I say, grinning at Sam.

Sam shrugs. "I'm just saying that we agreed to take turns. We did your playlist, and now we'll do mine."

Rachel rolls her eyes. "Does everything have to be so rational? *Goddamn.* You're totally a middle-aged dad."

Rachel exhales loudly and stomps away. But after a few steps, she turns around. "Hi, by the way," she says to me. "I'm glad you came. At least there's someone sane around here for a change."

Sam's sister can be a drama queen, but I actually like her. She's only a year younger than us, and she and Sam have most of the same friends. But the similarities end there. Where Sam is laid-back, Rachel gets hysterical about everything. Plus, she's kind of chunky and she's always giving herself these homemade tattoos and botched haircuts. It drives their mom crazy, which is another reason to like her.

Rachel was actually the reason Sam was at the hockey game the day I got hit. She was going out with the goalie and I think two-timing with the team manager. All her friends were hungover from a party the night before, so she dragged her brother along for company. I guess I have Rachel to thank for Sam. Or blame, depending on which state of mind I'm in.

"How's it going?" Sam asks, adjusting the volume on the speakers.

I shrug.

"Feeling better?"

Another shrug.

Sam turns down the bass and then steps closer to me. I breathe him in, all soapy and sexy. As we're kissing, I can feel the slightest hint of his tongue, so I part my lips wider and wrap my arms around his neck and then, all of a sudden, he pulls back and says, "Did you call your mom?"

"I still don't want to talk about that."

"I don't understand. . . ."

"Well, try to."

I turn away, but Sam reaches for my shoulder. "I'm sorry, okay?" he says. "Can we just let it go?"

"Okay." I sigh. "Let's just get this barbecue over with."

Sam frowns and I can tell I've hurt him. As we're heading toward the throng of Almonds, I reach for Sam's hand. I was meaning to give him an apologetic squeeze, but he takes it the wrong way and clutches on tight. I quickly liberate my hand, only I must have done it abruptly because he looks upset all over again. He shakes his head and mutters under his breath, and I know, I just know, that I shouldn't have come.

Sam didn't warn me about the aunts.

It turns out his mom has two sisters who are in town for the barbecue. They're basically clones of his mother, except they're even more famished for family gossip.

Sam's backyard is relatively large by Brockport standards. There's an in-ground pool in the middle and grassy areas on either side. On one side they have a table with gifts and framed class pictures of Sam from nursery school to senior year. Sam's mom has also displayed all of her scrapbooks, in case you wanted to glimpse Sam in his playpen or Sam in Little League or Sam on their backpacking trip through Japan last summer.

On the other side of the pool, they have a grill, lawn chairs, and a picnic table overflowing with food. Sam's mom has made lemon squares and frosted cookies shaped like caps and gowns. Sam's dad is sliding hot dogs and hamburgers onto a platter. But everyone is hovering around Sam's homemade wing dip, scooping the blend of shredded chicken, hot sauce, and cream cheese into their mouths with nacho chips.

Everyone, that is, except for the aunts. They're taking turns finding me, whenever I'm alone, and prying about Sam, my life history, Sam, Sam, and Sam. I've decided that while this backyard is large by Brockport standards, it's not large enough for the aunts and me.

In my first hour here, Aunt #1 wrangled out of me that I met Sam in March. Aunt #2 discovered it was at the hockey game. Aunt #1 circled back and started prying about the prom. Sam was getting us Cokes, but he returned in time to tell her we weren't into that sort of thing. When he said that, she clucked her tongue as if she were personally invested in dresses and tuxes and cheesy limo rides.

Around eight Sam and I are sitting by the pool, dunking our feet into the water. Rachel and her friend Janine are sprawled next to us, munching lemon squares and drawing peace signs on their thighs with a red Sharpie.

"Hey, Sam!" Sam's dad calls out. "I need some help with the grill."

"I'll be back," Sam says, touching my arm.

As soon as he's gone, Aunt #2 beelines over. "So," she says to me. "Tell me all about your college plans."

I flex my toes in the water. "I'm going to BU."

"My friend's daughter is in her second year at Simmons," she says. "She loves it! Her sister goes to MIT. So does her cousin."

Aunt #2 rambles on about how they're such brilliant kids, so talented, how Boston is such a great college town. By the time she's done talking, she's practically hoarse. I watch her walk over to her sister. They stand close to each other, chattering and nodding, and then Aunt #1 starts my way. I'm just bracing myself when Rachel taps my shoulder.

"Janine and I are going to go upstairs and drink a little," she whispers. "Want to come?"

I've been around Rachel enough to know that her drink of choice is Jack Daniel's, and when she can get someone to buy it for her, she stashes a bottle in her room.

"Sure," I say, grabbing my sandals and following her across the moist lawn.

As soon as we get upstairs, Janine locks the door and Rachel fetches a boot from the back of her closet. She fishes out a half-empty bottle, unscrews the top, and hands it to me.

I take a sip, swallow the burning in my throat, and then pass it to Janine. Rachel flops onto her bed and massages her temples. "Thank God for Jack," she moans. "My family is *craaaazy.*"

Janine hands the bottle to Rachel. "They don't seem so crazy?"

I don't know much about Janine except that everything out of her mouth sounds like a question and, according to Chastity Morgenstern, she once gave head to two football players at the same time, though I've never been able to figure out the logistics of that.

"Are you serious?" Rachel says, tossing back a shot. "If we had a family reunion, we'd have to wear shirts that said, THE ALMONDS: WE'RE ALL NUTS."

"Oh, my God!" Janine giggles. "That's so funny?"

"When can we leave for this party?" Rachel asks, handing the bottle back to me.

"Chastity told me it's not starting until nine or ten."

"Goddamn," Rachel says. "We are arriving at nine on the dot."

We pass around the bottle, and Rachel moans about how she's scared shitless because supposedly there'll be some hockey players coming to the party, including her ex-boyfriend and the guy she cheated on him with, and, basically, there's not enough alcohol in the world to settle her nerves in the next forty-five minutes.

Rachel takes one last swig, stuffs the bottle back into the boot, and then pulls a pack of black Twizzlers out of her dresser, tearing off a strip for each of us.

"Licorice?" I ask.

"For the breath," Rachel says. "My mom gets paranoid as soon as she smells mint."

On our way down the stairs, I feel light-headed and I stumble a little. I clutch my sandals in one hand and grab the banister with the other. As soon as we're outside, I spot Sam by the pool. I breathe in some fresh air and force myself to walk a straight line toward him.

"Licorice?" Sam asks as soon as we kiss. "Were you up in Rachel's room?"

I grin. "A little pre-game warm-up."

Sam is about to say something when Aunt #1 marches over and stands so close I can see the clogged pores rimming her nose.

"Do you know how far it is from Boston to Berkeley?" she asks.

"Huh?" Sam asks.

"More than three thousand miles," she says. "So how are you two going to stay together in the fall? I'm sure you've worked out a long-distance relationship plan, right?"

Sam and I glance at each other. And then, at the exact same second, we turn to his aunt and say:

Me: "We're not really together."

Sam: "We're talking about it."

Sam's aunt's mouth is hanging open so wide I can see the fillings in her teeth. But just as she begins to speak, Sam grabs my elbow and yanks me toward the edge of the yard.

"Why did you just say that?" he asks as soon as we're under the flowering white tree.

"Say what?"

Sam scowls. His cheeks are flushed and his face is strained, and, basically, I've never seen him look this angry.

"You mean that we're not together?" I ask.

Sam nods.

"It's not exactly *un*true. Besides, who cares what she thinks? She's just digging for gossip."

"I care," Sam says.

I watch as he clenches and unclenches his hands. The song playing on the laptop is this breathy ballad about a guy telling his girlfriend they fit together like puzzle pieces. We're definitely listening to Sam's playlist because on every one of his playlists, this song shows up.

"I'm so sick of all these rules with you," Sam says.

I lean down and peel a blade of grass off my ankle. "What rules?"

"*What rules?* We can't hold hands in public. We can't call each other boyfriend and girlfriend. We can't talk about the fall. Seriously, what the hell do you think is going to happen when we go to college? Do you want to just keep on hanging out this summer and then forget everything when you go to Boston?"

I have a feeling this is *not* the right time to tell him that, yes, that's exactly what I was thinking would happen. Instead, I say, "Can we please not talk about the future right now?"

"No, okay? I want to talk about it. I'm tired of you always saying what we can and can't talk about. And while we're at it, why don't you tell me exactly what you think we are, because I'm curious."

"I don't know what to . . ." I pause. If I had any buzz going on before, it's completely over now. "We're just having fun."

"I'm not having any fun," Sam says as he brushes a flower petal off the keyboard.

I reach over to touch Sam, but he jerks his arm away.

"Can we talk about this later?" I ask. "Let's get out of here, go to the party." I glance into the backyard. "Where're your sister and Janine?"

"You're not driving," Sam says flatly.

"What do you mean?"

"Weren't you drinking in Rachel's room? I'll drive your car and then just chill at the party."

"Whatever." I reach into my bra for my key. "But it's not like you're my mom."

"As if she'd care," Sam mutters.

My entire body goes cold.

"Fuck you," I say, chucking my key onto the ground and storming toward my car.

A few minutes later, as the four of us are heading down Hollybrook Lane, Sam and I still haven't said a word to each other. I'm sitting in the passenger seat, my hands tucked under my thighs, staring out the window. Sam is gripping the wheel, bouncing one of his knees up and down, and occasionally glancing in my direction.

As he flicks the blinker and turns onto Route 19, he says, "You told me the thing with your mom was no big deal."

I refuse to look at him.

"Just so you know," Sam says a few minutes later, "I actually *did* want to go to the prom."

I refuse to speak to him.

"What's going on?" Rachel asks from the backseat. "We're totally picking up on some tension."

When neither of us respond, she adds, "What's up with that hockey puck? It's staring right at me."

When we still don't respond, Rachel snorts. "I can see you two are going to have a blast at this party."

I continue staring out my window. Sam continues gripping the steering wheel.

4

As soon as we arrive, I head straight for the alcohol. Sam doesn't even come into the house with me. He cuts around to the back porch because some of his friends said they'd be there, most likely getting high. Generally that's where I'd be, too, except, first of all, I'm so mad I don't want to be anywhere near Sam and, second of all, weed makes me giggly. Since the last thing I want at this point is to giggle, I go in search of vodka.

Not that I'm this pothead alcoholic or anything. When I first got to Brockport, I smoked cigarettes and even stashed some weed in my room. My grandparents didn't know about the weed, but they jumped down my throat about the cigarettes. For the most part, I gave them up. By spring of junior year, I was so busy with a play and driver's ed and an SAT class, it was actually hard to find time to chill out.

But then, toward the end of last year, Aimee broke up with her surfer boyfriend and moved to Florida without telling me. I was really upset, and I smoked up with this drug-dealer guy at school and got suspended for the rest of the year. Naturally, my grandparents freaked out. We finally agreed that I'd give up the weed and they'd stop threatening to send me to rehab.

I haven't exactly told them I still smoke and drink at parties. The problem with my grandparents is they only see things in black and perfect, pristine white. Ever since my plane touched down last January, they've been on this mission to convert me to the perfect side of things. What they don't understand is that, first of all, they can do all the converting they want, but I'm still the same person deep down, and, second of all, you can be a good person and still have fun now and then.

Okay, I really need vodka.

Rachel and Janine disappear into the living room, where hip-hop is playing and girls are grinding and boys are drinking beer on the couch.

"Have you seen Chastity and Trinity?" I shout to some guy in the hallway.

"Who?"

"Identical twins."

"You mean Drunk and Drunker?" He waves his hand to the left. "They're in the kitchen."

As I'm heading down the hall, I pass these sliding doors that open into the backyard. Sure enough, there's

Sam and some other kids, sprawled in lawn chairs, smoking cigarettes and passing around what looks like a fat joint. I don't linger long enough to tell whether or not Sam is smoking because I don't want anyone to invite me out. I'm too mad to even *consider* talking to Sam right now. I understand he was angry, but he didn't have to corner me like that. And I can't believe what he said about my mom.

"V!" Trinity squeals. "What're you drinking?"

"Nothing yet," I say.

I glance around the kitchen table, where it looks like everyone used to be playing beer pong but now they're so drunk they're just sloshing balls into one another's cups. Trinity and Chastity are at one end, along with two guys I've never seen before. At the other end, there's the goalie that Rachel used to go out with, some red-haired girl, and Amos Harrington, who I've barely talked to since he brought me the puck the day after I got hit.

"Where's your other half?" Chastity asks, throwing a Ping-Pong ball in my direction.

"What other half?" I ask.

Trinity and Chastity glance at each other.

"You need to get drunk," Trinity says.

As she wobbles over to the counter to mix me a vodka and cranberry, I scoop up the ball and toss it toward Amos. He catches it with both hands.

I pull up a chair between the twins, and for the next hour or so, we drink and chat and flick balls around the table. People wander in and out of the kitchen. Rachel and

Janine appear in the doorway, but as soon as they see Rachel's ex, they rush back down the hall. I finish my drink, and Trinity makes me another. I can feel Amos smiling at me. My face is flushed, but I'm feeling good. I'm having fun. I reach across Trinity and splash a little more vodka in my cup.

By this point Chastity is sitting on one of the guy's laps. His name is Gavin. His hands are inching closer and closer to her boobs, and whenever they kiss, they're making these sucky-slurpy noises.

"Hey, Chas," Trinity says sleepily. "That's what beds are for."

We all crack up. I can feel Amos watching me. I pull my hair back from my face and twist it into a loose knot.

After a while Chastity and Gavin go in search of a free bedroom. Once they're gone Trinity rests her face on the table and closes her eyes. The red-haired girl and the goalie head toward the living room, trailed closely by the other guy. Which leaves Amos and me at opposite ends of the table, rolling a dented ball back and forth.

Damn.

This is dangerous.

"Where's the bathroom?" I stand up and brace myself against the counter.

"I'll show you," Amos says, pushing back his chair.

Damn.

I forgot how hot he is. Stocky but muscular.

Damn.

I am way too drunk for this.

"You don't have to get all . . ." I'm trying to remember that word for a guy doting on a girl and opening doors for her, but my brain is so fuzzy the only thing I can think about is how Amos and I hooked up at that party in March and he grabbed me toward him, pressing his lips hard against mine.

"I don't have to get all what?" Amos whispers in my ear.

We're standing an inch from each other, and it's obvious there's lust going on. I can feel it between my legs, and as Amos steps closer to me, I can feel it between his legs, too.

"You're looking hot tonight," Amos says.

His breath smells like alcohol and wet cigarettes, but it's okay. In fact, it's turning me on.

"Bathroom?" I ask meekly. My hair slips out of the knot and falls past my shoulders.

Amos takes my arm and steers me through the dining room and into the bathroom. Before I can say anything, he's inside with me and I'm locking the door and we're making out. I'm leaning against the sink and we're rubbing our bodies together and he's grabbing my boobs and I'm grabbing his butt and he's just reaching down to unzip his jeans when someone knocks at the door.

"Hey!" a voice shouts.

I jerk away from Amos. *Shit.* It's not just a voice. It's Rachel Almond.

"Chastity and some guy are in the other bathroom," Rachel wails. "If you know Chastity, you know how long they're going to take, so please let me in. I'm going to keep knocking until whoever's in there opens this door."

I can feel my stomach churning. I can feel saliva pooling under my tongue.

"Amos." I push him toward the door. "I'm going to throw up."

"Want me to hold your hair?"

"I don't think so."

Amos unlocks the door and I press myself against the towel rack so Rachel won't see me. But as soon as Amos mumbles that there's still another person in there, Rachel flicks the light switch and peers inside.

"V?" she asks in this horrified voice.

For a second, we both just stand there, staring at each other. Then she turns and disappears through the dining room.

I close the door and sink onto my knees in front of the toilet bowl. I attempt to puke, but nothing comes out. I can't believe how drunk I am. I can't believe I just fooled around with Amos. I can't believe Rachel saw us. I can't believe my mom didn't come to graduation. I know deep down she doesn't love me, but I guess I'm always hoping for her to prove that wrong.

I slump against the bathtub, sobbing. Someone bangs on the door. I keep crying and eventually they go away.

After a while I wipe my face with some toilet paper and wander out of the bathroom. I grab my sandals from where I'd slipped them off under the kitchen table and stumble through the house.

As soon as I get outside, I see my car parked on the grass. I know for a fact I'm in no shape to drive. Besides, Sam has the key. Even so, I check the doors. The back is unlocked, so I toss my sandals onto the floor, grab my phone, and walk down the empty street.

5

I hear a car pulling in the driveway. It's pitch-dark. I'm not really awake, not really sleeping. Mostly, I'm just gripping the edges of my mattress, trying to keep the room from spinning, trying not to heave up whatever is sloshing around in my stomach.

I fumble on my bedside table for my phone. The light from the screen pierces my eyes. No missed calls. No voice mails. No text messages. I moan and drop my phone onto the bed.

I hear an engine cutting out. I hear a car door opening. Is it Sam? Should I go down and talk to him? What would I say? *Thanks for returning my car. It was nice knowing you. Sorry I fucked everything up.*

I hear a car door close. I hoist myself out of bed, but the second I'm upright my stomach seizes. I barely make it to the bathroom in time to puke my guts into the toilet.

*   *   *

"V?"

It's bright out, brutally bright, and the doorbell is ringing. My clock says 7:14 A.M., but it's way too bright to be 7:14 A.M. Besides, who would ring the doorbell at this brutal, brutal hour?

"V?"

My grandma is at the bottom of the stairs that lead up to my room. This used to be the guest room, but I've been staying here ever since last January. It actually took me eight months to unpack my bags. But once I learned that Aimee had moved to Florida, and my grandparents convinced me to stay here for senior year, I folded my clothes into drawers, taped up some photos, and bought a beanbag chair. It probably doesn't sound like a big deal to most people, but to me, at the time, it was huge.

I press my face into a pillow. My temples are pounding even worse than last night.

"There's someone at the door for you," my grandma is saying.

Oh, my God.

Is it Sam?

Oh, my God.

"It's the FedEx guy," my grandma adds. "I think something from Aimee."

I mumble that I'll get it later and then burrow my face deep into the pillow.

*   *   *

"V?"

My grandma is back at the bottom of the stairs.

"We're heading to work," my grandpa chimes in.

I attempt to open my eyes, but it's even brighter than before.

"She must be sleeping still," my grandma murmurs.

"I'll call her later," my grandpa says. "See if she wants to have lunch."

Argh.

My grandma works in Rochester, so I'm off her radar most of the day, but my grandpa is a dentist in Brockport, which means he's constantly inviting me to have lunch with him or go for afternoon power walks on the canal.

"That sounds good," my grandma says. "I know she had a hard time yesterday."

As their footsteps recede down the hall, I turn onto my side, hug my knees to my chest, and fall back asleep.

My phone is ringing, but I can't find it anywhere.

I glance at the clock: 10:23 A.M.

The ring tone is this tinny version of "The Battle Hymn of the Republic." Sam put it on there a few days ago, after I snuck "Oh, Shenandoah" onto his phone. I know it was funny in the moment, but when you're just waking up from the worst hangover of your life, the last thing you want to hear is "The Battle Hymn of the Republic," courtesy of the guy you just cheated on.

I finally discover my phone wedged between the sheet and the side of my mattress. Just as I'm opening it, the ringing stops. I glance at the last call. AIMEE. I quickly dial her back.

"Hey!" my mom says. "I just tried you."

"I know. I was sleeping."

"Want to call me when you're awake?"

"No . . . that's okay." I fold an extra pillow under my head. "What's up?"

"I just wanted to say I'm *so* sorry about missing your graduation. We went back to the emergency room in the middle of the night for more testing, but they sent us home again and . . . Oh, hon, I really am sorry. You know how much I wanted to see you walk across that stage."

I'm getting the hugest lump in my throat.

"Did my package arrive?" Aimee asks.

I remember brightness, a searing headache, my grandma shouting from the bottom of the stairs.

"It should have come this morning," Aimee says. "It's lots of stuff for college. I was going to bring it with me to Brockport."

My eyes are filling with tears.

"Speaking of college," Aimee says, "I was thinking I could use my ticket to fly back east in August. We could rent a car and I'll drive you to Boston, get you settled in. What do you think?"

"That sounds nice."

We're both quiet for a moment. Then I wipe my eyes and say, "What's his name, by the way?"

"The Cowboy?"

"Yeah."

"Steve," Aimee says. "And do you want to know something? We're talking about buying a house together, maybe even a ranch."

"In San Antonio?"

"Yeah . . . you should come visit."

"Really?"

"You'd like it here. Steve has three horses that he boards in a nearby stable."

"Horses?"

"We could take them out whenever you want."

I say that sounds nice, even though riding a horse around Texas was not exactly what I had in mind for myself this summer.

Twenty minutes later I'm down in the kitchen sucking a saltine and wondering whether Rachel told Sam that she saw me with Amos. I'm sure she did because Sam hasn't called or texted yet, and we've never gone this long after an argument. Then again, I've never cheated on him before. But I can't *really* call it cheating because we never made any monogamy pledges.

The home phone rings.

"Hello?" I ask.

"Hey," Mara says. "I heard."

"Heard what?"

"About graduation . . . Mom and Dad told me about Aimee not showing up."

"That was fast."

"You know them," she says. "They're talking about sending you to therapy this summer."

"At least it's not rehab this time."

"Seriously," Mara says, laughing.

Mara is my grandparents' other daughter. Officially, that makes her my aunt, except they had Mara when Aimee was eighteen, so she's only a year older than me. When I moved here last year, Mara was a senior. She was this super-uptight, perfectionist overachiever, and I was, well, the opposite. At first we wanted to murder each other, but things got better throughout that spring. By the time Mara left for Yale in August, I'd even say we liked each other.

"Are you okay?" Mara asks.

I snort. "Hardly."

"How so?"

"I fucked things up with Sam."

"Oh no," Mara says, and I can hear genuine regret in her voice. She's spending the summer in Chicago, but she was home for five days after Yale let out. While she was here, she hung around with Sam and me a few times and kept saying how she'd never seen me that happy.

"What happened?" Mara asks.

I tell her about the fight, the party, Amos.

"That sounds awful," Mara says.

"I know."

"Do you think you guys are over?"

"It can't be over because it never was anything to begin with."

"You really believe that?"

"Hmmm," I say. "I guess I'll have to discuss it with my therapist."

"Stop joking. I know you're upset."

I pour myself some Dr Pepper, but my stomach is still too queasy, so I dump it into the sink and fill my glass with water.

"Have you talked to Aimee yet?" Mara asks.

"Yeah . . . she FedExed me this package, all these body scrubs and picture frames for my dorm room. She even sent a lava lamp. That's nice, right?"

"I guess," Mara says.

I'm sipping some water when I realize my temples are pounding. I tell Mara I'll call her later and then gulp a few Advil and head upstairs to my room. I grab a marker off my desk, write I HATE MYSELF on the back of my hand, and crawl into bed. I attempt to fall asleep but no matter what, I can't get "The Battle Hymn of the Republic" out of my head.

6

Sam is everywhere.

Over the next four days, I can't step out of the house without seeing him trimming the shrubs across the street. Well, not him. But for a second, I think it's him and my pulse starts racing and I wonder whether I should say hi. But then I realize it's actually our neighbor, who also happens to be a middle-aged Korean woman, and I don't know whether to be relieved or disappointed.

I see Sam as I'm driving to Pizza Hut. He's taking a right onto State Street and, for some reason, behind the wheel of a mail truck.

I see Sam as I'm delivering a pan pizza to a table by the door. He's hunched over the gumball machine, forcing in some coins. But then I look closer and discover it's a pre-pubescent boy with braces and a botched crew cut.

I see Sam as I'm driving home from Pizza Hut. This time I swear it's him, and I practically mow down two cars to catch up. But once I'm on his fender, I realize he's got a pancake-size bald spot and a car seat in the back.

That's pretty much all I've been doing. Driving to Pizza Hut, thinking I see Sam, waiting tables, thinking I see Sam, driving home, thinking I see Sam. During the hours I'm not working, my grandparents leave for their offices and I stay in bed for as long as possible and then watch TV for as many hours as possible and then, when I can't stand it any longer, I check my phone for calls from Sam. Of course, there's never anything, so I linger in front of the fridge for as long as possible and then stay in the shower until I'm as wrinkly as possible and then, when I can't stand it any longer, I check my buddy list to see if Sam is online or, at the very least, if he's posted some revealing away message. Of course, there's never anything, so I climb back in bed or turn on the TV or graze in the fridge or paint my fingernails and then chip everything off and then paint them all over again.

On Friday evening, four days after what I now refer to as The Night I Fucked Everything Up, I'm just settling down on the couch when I hear my grandparents whispering in the kitchen. I have this telepathic sense they're about to lasso me into a Family Meeting, so I grab my flip-flops, shout that I'm taking a walk, and hurry out the side door.

When I reach the end of the driveway, I consider turning right on Centennial, except that would send me in the direction of Sam's house. I consider going straight down

Chapel, except Sam's friend Luca lives there and sometimes they go cycling together in the evenings. So I take a left and cross the intersection. I walk through the middle-school parking lot, over the track, past the grid of yellow buses, all the way to the high school.

There are three or four cars in the parking lot. Someone has propped open the pool door with a brick, probably a janitor on a smoke break. I hesitate for a second and then slip inside. As I wander the empty halls, littered with rusty apple cores and battered notebooks, I'm overwhelmed by the scent of chlorine and French fries and something else, probably hormones, but it doesn't kick in the slightest trace of nostalgia. Not that I was expecting any. I went to Brockport High longer than anywhere else, but by the time I got here, I'd attended seventeen different schools. Some were longer, like when I did all of third grade in Seattle, but that was balanced out by the time Aimee moved us to Bangor, Maine, for twelve days. That was in seventh grade. We arrived in early December and were crashing in a motel while Aimee scouted for longer-term accommodations. But then, when she picked me up from school one Wednesday, she announced that Maine was too damn cold. We checked out of the motel the following morning, did Christmas with my grandparents and Mara, and then drove to South Carolina for the winter.

I pass Sam's locker and suddenly remember all those times we used to meet here between periods. I'm especially remembering last Thursday, when I was helping Sam clean out this very locker. We were returning from a trash run when we discovered a neon-pink Super Soaker someone had left behind. We filled it up in a water fountain and got into this huge war on our way to the student parking lot. Of course, we ended up having to go to his house to change and, of course, changing involves taking off your clothes, which I guess was the point in the first place.

I spin around, hurry back through the hallways, and push open the pool door. Just as I'm stepping onto the path, I trip, go flying, and smack down hard on the concrete, ripping the hell out of my right knee.

That fucking brick, I think as the blood trickles down my shin. I limp over to the lawn area, wincing in pain. I stay there for a long time, watching the sky turn pink and orange. It would actually be beautiful if I weren't slumped on the edge of a parking lot, wiping blood off my leg and smearing it onto the grass.

It doesn't help that my grandparents are obsessed with the idea that I need therapy. It started on Tuesday evening, the day after The Night I Fucked Everything Up. It was obviously they'd been scheming all day because the second they saw me, they were like, "We know you're upset about what happened with Aimee. We'll get referrals for therapists, so just let us know if you'd feel more comfortable with a woman or a man. Younger or older? And are you okay driving into Rochester by yourself?"

Then, on Wednesday evening, they tag-teamed me again and asked about Sam and why weren't they seeing him around. When I told them it was over, my grandpa shook his head and said, "This is *just* the sort of thing to explore in therapy."

My grandpa touched my arm. "You know, sweetie, a woman probably makes sense, especially if you'll be talking about . . . errr . . . romantic issues."

On Thursday night I dragged Chastity and Trinity into Gates for a movie and then forced them to drink coffee with me at Common Grounds until it was well past the hour when my grandparents went to bed.

But on Friday night, when I returned home with that bloody knee, my grandparents were like, "Aaaah! Self-mutilation!"

"I tripped on a brick," I said to them. "I just need some Band-Aids."

Even as they hovered over my leg, squeezing on the Neosporin, they still acted suspicious, as if I had plunged to the pavement to act out repressed anger that I needed to address in therapy.

So this is why, as I'm sitting at the breakfast nook on Sunday morning, I have my headphones on. I just want to send that extra signal that I'm not available for conversation right now.

"V?" My grandpa presses his hands onto my shoulders. "Grandma and I would like to have a Family Meeting."

"Huh?" I ask.

"FAMILY! MEETING!"

"Oh."

"Now."

My grandparents settle onto the couch. I sit in the comfy chair. They start by saying how things have gotten so much better since I arrived in Brockport and how they're proud of my accomplishments, but they've suspected all along that I've got some issues from my past still haunting me, so when Aimee didn't show up for graduation and they saw the effect it had on me, it made them think I'd benefit from a summer of therapy.

I have no idea where to even *begin* defending myself. When they're done, I just say, "Things are actually okay with Aimee now. We talked on Tuesday and she sent me that package. Plus, she's going to fly out here at the end of the summer and drive me to Boston."

My grandparents stare at me.

"Aimee even said I could visit her in Texas this summer," I quickly add.

My grandparents exchange this skeptical look, and then my grandpa says, "Do you really think Aimee will make it in August?"

"I hope so," I say.

"How are you doing about Sam?" my grandma asks.

I gulp hard. Should I tell them how I've been imagining I see him everywhere? Should I tell them how, as I was tossing in bed this morning, I remembered what his skin smells like after he's been in the sun? On Senior Ditch Day last month, a bunch of us went to this quarry and drank beer and swung on a rope into the chilly water. In the late afternoon, Sam and I cuddled on a blanket and he stretched his arm around me and I rested my head on his chest and oh, my God, his skin smelled salty and sweaty and just so . . . so *not* what I feel like telling my grandparents.

"We have the name of a wonderful therapist," my grandma says. "Her name is Alana. She's in Fairport, but it sounds like she's worth the drive."

"We talked with her yesterday," my grandpa adds, "told her a little about your situation. She's expecting to hear from you soon."

I spring to my feet. "What?"

"We said you'd call her this weekend or early next week," my grandma says.

"But I don't want to see a therapist. I know you think that'd be good for me, but I—"

"We saw," my grandpa says.

My grandma nods solemnly.

What are they talking about? They saw the condom stash in the back of my makeup drawer? They installed a microscopic camera in my brain and saw me with Amos at that party?

My grandpa sighs heavily and then explains how on Tuesday afternoon he drove home to see if I wanted to have lunch, but he couldn't find me anywhere so he came up to my room and saw me sleeping and there was that I HATE MYSELF written on my hand. They were planning to address it with me that night, but by the time they got home, I'd washed it off and they didn't want it to seem like they were invading my privacy, but since I'm refusing to consider therapy, they feel they must express their concerns.

"I've got to get out of here," I say, grabbing my phone and storming out the door.

My immediate reaction is to call Sam. That's what I think as I sink into an Adirondack chair in the backyard. Of course, that's out of the question, so I consider trying Chastity, but then I remember that she and Trinity are on a plane to Daytona Beach for a monthlong volleyball program.

I hug my thighs to my chest. Things are seriously sucking right now. At this point I just want my old self back. It's not like everything was perfect before I met Sam, but I wasn't this miserable, either.

I open my phone and dial Amos. We didn't have the smoothest good-bye at that party, but I have a feeling he won't mind hearing from me.

"Hello?"

"Amos . . . it's V."

"What's up, V? It's Henry."

"Henry?"

"Amos's brother."

"Oh," I say, remembering that time in March when Amos and I were fooling around in his bedroom and his brother kept inventing reasons to knock on the door until Amos threatened to beat the shit out of him if he didn't stay away. He was younger, like ninth grade, and hadn't yet learned that if you stare unblinkingly at a girl's boobs, you look like a pervert.

"What's up?" Henry asks.

"Didn't I call Amos's phone?"

"Yeah . . . but he's camping, so he loaned it to me."

"When's he getting back?"

"You're the girl who got hit by the hockey puck, right?"

"Yeah."

"That's sexy."

"Sexy?"

"All that blood and—"

"When's Amos getting back?"

"Next week." Henry says. "But I'm—"

"Okay," I say. "Well, thanks."

"Now that I have your number, can I—"

"Bye!" I shout, quickly pressing the END button.

After I hang up, I scroll through my phone book until I find Brandon Parker. He's that guy I smoked up with at school last spring. We haven't talked since then because while I got suspended, he got expelled. It wasn't the first time he'd been caught, not to mention he was one of the major suppliers of drugs to the youth of western New York.

Brandon's mom answers the phone. When I ask for him, she says, "Didn't you know?"

"Know what?" I ask. I'm imagining prison or rehab.

"Brandon joined the army. He's in the Middle East. Would you like a yellow ribbon?"

"A yellow ribbon?"

"To show support for Brandon. Or a pin with his picture on it? Whatever you want. Just tell me where you live, and I'll drop everything off in an hour."

I have to say yes. I have to give her my address. When her minivan pulls into our driveway, I have to hug her and make a big display of stroking the yellow ribbon and pinning Brandon's face on my chest.

As soon as she's gone, I chuck everything into the kitchen trash, right on top of a coffee filter. But then I start worrying about karma and how mine is already in the negative numbers, so I dig out the pin, rinse off the coffee grounds, and vow to wear it on my shirt for the rest of the day.

"Who's that soldier?" the new dishwasher asks as he stabs an oily finger toward my boob. His name is Russell, and he's been checking me out since he started here in May.

It's Sunday evening. We've just gotten through the dinner rush, and I'm leaning against the door to the freezer, chugging watery fountain soda.

Tonight has sucked so far. A pack of preteens dominated my section, sending back their pizzas, unscrewing the Parmesan shakers, and stiffing me on a tip. Not to mention that my phone kept vibrating in my pocket and I kept leaping for it, but it always said AMOS, which meant it was Henry, wanting to talk dirty about blood.

"That soldier isn't her boyfriend," says a server named Linda. She's a single mom in her forties, and we've gotten pretty friendly with each other. "V's with that tall guy. Haven't you seen them together?"

"We're not together," I say. "I mean, we weren't together. But it doesn't matter. It's over."

"You and Sam?" Linda asks, her face all concerned.

"So you're with that solider now?" Russell asks.

"Not him, either." I dump my cup into the sink and head into the dining room.

A few minutes later, as I'm reciting the pan-pizza special to a middle-aged couple, I glance out the window and spot Sam cycling toward West Avenue. This time it's definitely him. I recognize the slope of his shoulders and that navy-blue shirt I once snuck out of his room and wore to bed every night for a week.

The man asks me which five toppings he can add to the special pizza. I'm so disturbed I repeat green peppers twice and completely blank on sausage and mushrooms.

As I stumble into the kitchen, Linda touches my arm. "You okay?" she asks. "You look pale."

I shake my head and say I'm fine, but Linda insists on bringing them their raspberry iced teas so I can pull myself together.

As soon as she's gone, Russell tosses a congealed slice

of pepperoni into his mouth. "Want to go to the parking lot for a smoke break?"

Russell has a graveyard of crooked teeth and no apparent chin. Normally, I would blow him off, but I could use the distraction right now. I set down my pad and follow him outside.

It's a humid night, still dusky even though it's almost nine. There's a couple making out in a junky car on the other side of the parking lot. They're seriously going at it, groping hands, steamy windows, the occasional flash of flabby skin.

"Want one?" Russell asks, shaking a cigarette out of a pack and handing it to me.

"Thanks," I say, leaning into him as he holds up a lighter.

As Russell sucks his cigarette and blabbers about the Zen of scrubbing pizza pans, I stare at West Avenue and wonder where Sam was going on his bike and whether he saw my car as he pedaled past Pizza Hut.

"What happened to your knee?" Russell asks, blowing smoke out of the corner of his mouth.

I glance down at my black pants. "My knee?"

"I saw that scab. You were wearing a skirt when you came in . . . before you changed."

"Oh," I say. "I tripped."

Russell grins. "You sure it didn't have anything to do with your soldier?"

"I really tripped," I say. "Fuck you, by the way."

"Sounds good to me."

I look out at West Avenue again. I wonder if Sam is going to be cycling back anytime soon. *Holy shit!* What if he loops around and sees me smoking with Russell in the parking lot?

I drop my cigarette onto the concrete. "I better go check my tables."

"That's cool," Russell says. "We should do this again."

As I turn to head inside, he swats my butt with his greasy fingers.

Great.

So now I've got Russell's pepperoni on my ass. I've got Brandon's face on my chest. I've got Amos's brother sitting on his REDIAL button. I've got a disgusting scab on my knee. I've got a therapist waiting for my call. And I still can't forget. And Sam is still everywhere.

7

On Monday afternoon I drive to Wegmans to buy pasta-salad ingredients. Today is July fourth. When I was growing up, Aimee used to make pasta salad every summer, with broccoli and olives and Good Seasons dressing. I'm not a culinary goddess by any stretch of the imagination. Actually, my idea of cooking doesn't involve a stove, boiling water, or anything that has to be chopped, but my grandparents were hovering around the house all day, trying to convince me that therapy is what I need. Finally, I announced my mission to make pasta salad.

As I'm pulling into the parking lot, I dial Aimee. Whenever I call her, a little part of me is nervous that her phone will be disconnected. Every time she moves, she trades in her old number and gets one with the current area code. But if she doesn't call me with the new information, I actually have no way of getting in touch with her, other than e-mail, which she rarely checks. That's how it was for five days last fall, when Aimee moved to the Georgia coast.

"This is Aimee Valentine," Aimee's voice says. "Leave me a message and I'll get back to you as soon as I can."

I tell Aimee's voice mail that I'm making pasta salad and I need to double-check the recipe. Then I lock my car, push my sunglasses onto my nose, and head into Wegmans.

I forgot to grab a cart, so I'm cradling a box of noodles, the salad-dressing packet, and a can of olives. Then I cruise over to produce, where I stare at the vegetable displays. I know I need broccoli, but I'm blanking on the other ingredients. *Celery? Onions?* I wish Aimee would call me back already.

"Hey, V."

I spin around and I'm face-to-face with Rachel Almond. I'm so freaked out, I drop the olives.

Rachel and I watch the can roll toward the onions and garlic, and then stare up at each other. My cheeks flush when I remember the last time I saw her. She looks embarrassed, too. She crooks her head to one side, stubs her sandal against the floor, and says, "So . . . what's up?"

I glance into her basket, filled with bottles of Gatorade, energy bars, and two containers of strawberries. On her left wrist, she has a temp tattoo that says LOVELY surrounded by a rainbow and a sprinkling of hearts.

Rachel gestures toward her groceries. "We're about to take the kayaks on the canal . . . going down to my uncle's in Spencerport."

"You and Sam?" I ask.

As soon as I say that, I feel all sweaty and anxious, like I have to pee and I'm going to cry and I want to run except my feet are stuck in place. Rachel's mouth is doing this twitchy thing, which I instantly interpret as *Sam is actually on his way over here right now,* which sends me into an instant panic because I've been "seeing" Sam everywhere this past week, but I still haven't figured out what I'd say if I actually *saw* him.

All of a sudden, I understand why Aimee ditches town, state, and time zone after a breakup. She, unlike me, knows that to hang around will inevitably lead to messy encounters, and, honestly, that's the last thing you want when you go to the grocery store to buy ingredients for pasta salad.

After a long pause, Rachel says, "No . . . just me and my mom. She's on this agonizing kick to improve our mother-daughter relationship."

"Oh," I say, rubbing my nose and staring at the ground.

Rachel shifts her weight from one foot to the other. Then she reaches down, picks up the can of olives, and hands it to me.

"I probably shouldn't be telling you this," she says, "but Sam is in California. He left on Friday morning."

"*What?*"

"He found a last-minute house share, and I think he has an interview lined up at a bakery."

"But I thought . . ."

"I don't know, V. You know about my history with the hockey boys, so I'm hardly in a position to judge. But I can't *believe* you did that to Sam. You guys were more than that. After that . . . after that night . . . I don't think I've ever seen my brother so wrecked. He said it was too hard to be in Brockport after you . . . after you . . ."

I can feel the tears coming. I mumble that I have to go, and then I rush past the bananas, past the Chinese food buffet, past the piles of corn. Once I hit the parking lot, I realize I'm still clutching my groceries. I set everything onto a curb, hoping one of those pimply guys who collects the shopping carts will bring it all back inside.

Then I just stand there, squinting because it's so bright and I can't find my sunglasses and my hands are too slick to grip my keys and I can't even remember where I parked my car.

I sink onto the curb, lower my head between my knees, and cry. For the past week, Sam has been everywhere in Brockport. But he's not here. And I didn't even know. And it's really over.

I'm just unlocking my car when my phone rings. I reach down and grab it out of my bag. AIMEE.

"Hello?" I ask as I unlock the door and slide onto the scalding hot seat.

"Spiral noodles, of course, and that yummy salad-dressing mix, steamed broccoli, olives, minced red onion, and a bell pepper. Oh, and don't forget the Parmesan."

I wipe my eyes with my hand.

"Everything okay?" Aimee asks.

I start crying all over again.

"What's going on, baby?"

I fish a crumpled paper towel off the floor and blow my nose. "You remember Sam, right?"

"The guy who caught you after the hockey puck."

"Well, I screwed everything up with him and I just ran into his sister and I'm a horrible person and . . ." I lapse into another round of tears.

"Maybe Sam wasn't right for you," Aimee says. "Besides, you're going to college in a few months, so why get too invested in anything at this point?"

"Grandma and Grandpa are threatening to send me to therapy," I say, sniffling.

Aimee groans.

"What?" I ask.

"They wanted to send me, too."

"When?"

"When I told them I was dropping out of college and moving to Colorado to become a ski instructor."

"That's where you . . ."

"Exactly," Aimee says. "Where I met the Sperm Donor."

Aimee rarely talks about my father, and when she does, she just calls him the Sperm Donor. I've learned over the years that his name is Brian. He played guitar, smoked a lot of weed, and lived on the slopes. Aimee has hinted that he never knew about me because by the time her pregnancy was showing, she'd moved to a vineyard in northern California.

"I'm not saying if I'd gone to therapy, I wouldn't have had you," Aimee says.

"But maybe, right?"

"Basically," Aimee concludes, "it's better I didn't go."

I can feel myself choking up. I've never deluded myself into thinking I was a planned teenage pregnancy, but it's nice to know I'm not altogether unwanted.

"You should come to Texas," Aimee says. "Have you thought any more about that?"

"That'd really be okay?"

"Are you kidding? Steve and I can show you around San Antonio. You'd love it. Everyone calls each other *ya'll* out here."

"How would I get there?"

"You could fly," Aimee says. "Steve and I are saving for a house, so money's tight around here. Want me to talk to Grandpa about getting your ticket?"

I consider this for a moment. I can just hear them saying, *Think about how Aimee always lets you down, V. Wouldn't the money be better spent talking to a therapist?* Besides, I've got my Pizza Hut savings and that cash from the theater award at graduation, so I could probably scrape together enough for a plane ticket.

"Let me think about it," I say.

"Sure . . . but you say the word and I'll call Grandpa."

"Thanks."

"I actually have to run," Aimee says. "You wouldn't believe it, but I'm just boiling noodles for *my* pasta salad."

"Okay . . . well, thanks for talking."

"Anytime," Aimee says.

After we hang up, I get this aching feeling inside as I think about how much I'd like to be eating pasta salad with my mom today.

Maybe I'll drive to Texas.

That's what I think on my way home from Wegmans. Well, not home. My grandparents' house. That's what I'm thinking about, too. Ever since last summer, I started calling this place home. But it's really not. It's where I've been crashing because I haven't had any other place to go. But now Aimee has invited me to San Antonio. That's not home, either. But maybe I'm one of those people who shouldn't attempt the whole home thing in the first place.

Look what it's done to me in Brockport. I grew way too comfortable here, way too soft. A few years ago, I never would have gotten so caught up in one guy. But now I'm this sobbing wreck, and even though Sam's no longer here, everything in Brockport reminds me of him.

I need to get out of town.

I guess I could fly to Texas. I'm sure that's what my

grandparents would want me to do. But if I'm going to use my money for this trip, I should do it *my* way, right? Not their way, all pampered and protected like some delicate princess.

Honestly, I don't even *deserve* to be pampered. What I deserve is to be driving through the middle of nowhere, surrounded by cornfields or cabbage fields or whatever they have between here and Texas. I deserve to sleep in roadside motels where no one attempts to hug me good night. I deserve to speed along interstates and have no one know whether or not I'm safe. And if something awful *does* happen, I don't want anyone around to make it better.

That, at least, will feel familiar.

By the time I turn onto Centennial, my decision is made. I'm going to drive to Texas.

8

When I get back to the house, I hurry straight to the computer and research my plans. The distance between Brockport and San Antonio, using the route I want, is 1,850 miles. If I drive 370 miles every day, it will take about five days. So that means I could leave Brockport one morning and stay in a motel somewhere in Ohio that first night. Then I'd drive through Chicago and sleep over with Mara, before heading down to St. Louis, where I'd do another motel. Aimee has some friends in Springfield, Missouri, so I could see if they'd take me in for a night. Then a motel in Oklahoma and, from there, I'd head down through Texas. So that makes three or four motels and seven or eight tanks of gas and I guess food and tolls. I check my bank account. If I don't spend money on anything stupid, I definitely have enough for the trip.

By the time I sit down with my grandparents that afternoon, I've prepared every answer under the sun. But when I announce that I'm driving to San Antonio, my grandpa leans back on the couch, crosses his arms over his chest, and says, "Absolutely not."

My grandma shakes her head. "I really don't think that's a good idea."

"It's not just a bad idea," my grandpa says. "It's out of the question."

"Can I at least tell you my plans?" I can feel the anger pulsing down my arms. At least they have to hear me out before they shoot me down. "I could divide up the trip enough so I'd only drive during the day. And I'd get a good map, so I wouldn't have to ask strangers for directions. And I'd have my cell phone, so I could call—"

"This isn't even worth talking about," my grandpa says. "There's no way you can handle almost two thousand miles of highway driving. You haven't even had your license for a year."

"But you let me drive to Syracuse for that show. That's over a hundred miles on the highway. This is basically like going back and forth to Syracuse eighteen times."

"Honey," my grandma says, "this is a little different than driving to Syracuse . . ."

"Aimee *really* invited you to Texas?" my grandpa asks.

"Are you saying I'm lying?" I snap. By this point I'm not just angry. I'm *furious*. "Are you saying she doesn't want me to visit her? Because as much as you might like that to be true, you're wrong."

"We just think after what happened at graduation . . ." My grandpa pauses. "Maybe these things would be better discussed in thera—"

Goddamn!

I storm up to my room and slam the door. But the fighting is far from over. We have another round on Tuesday morning before they leave for work. That night, when they still won't listen, I finally inform them that they're not my legal guardians, so they can't actually tell me what to do. When I say that, my grandma turns pale and my grandpa says, "So we'll call Aimee and ask her. I'm sure she'll agree with us."

He plucks up the phone and marches onto the side porch.

Aimee ends up giving me the green light. Later that night she recounts to me how she told my grandpa that when she was my age, she was practically a mother, so what's a little cross-country drive? I tell her I'll probably leave Sunday or Monday and arrive by the following weekend.

On Wednesday I give notice at Pizza Hut. On Thursday I bring my car in for an oil change and a tune-up. On Friday I go to Lift Bridge Book Shop and get a spiral-bound atlas. On Saturday I buy Pringles and pretzels and energy bars to eat on the road.

I e-mail Mara in Chicago and Aimee's friends in Springfield. Every time I sit at the computer, I try not to obsess about how I still haven't heard from Sam. Of course, I fail miserably and end up reading old conversations we had online until my eyes are bugging and I'm so depressed I want to die.

One afternoon my grandma goes to Dick's Sporting Goods and comes home with supplies for my trip. As she presents me with a Swiss Army knife, a compass, a cooler, and a zero-degree sleeping bag, I have a hard time disguising my amusement. A zero-degree sleeping bag? Because the Midwest in July is so frigid? And a compass? I'm only taking major interstates, so it's not like I'll be bumping down dirt roads, searching for the magnetic North Pole.

"Sweetie," my grandma says as she tucks everything back into the bag, "you're coming home after this, right?"

"Yeah," I say. I just don't mention that I've recently realized I have no idea where my home actually is.

"And college is still on?"

"Of course."

"This may sound like a strange question," my grandma says after a minute, "but what are you looking for out there?"

I stare at her. For the first time in four days, I don't have an answer. To be perfectly honest, I have no idea what I'm looking for out there. And I have a feeling my new compass won't help me find it.

*   *   *

On my last night at Pizza Hut, Linda gives me all her tips.

"For your drive," she says, her espresso-brown eyes filling with tears.

"No way."

I try to hand back the envelope of cash, but she shakes her head. "I've also written down my cousin's number for you. He and his wife live in Erie, right on the lake. Really nice people. They have two children, a little older than you. I called Darren this morning and told him about you. He said you're welcome to sleep over at their house anytime."

"You didn't have to do that."

Linda wipes her mascara smudges with the side of her finger. "I wish I knew people all the way across the country."

I tuck the envelope into my bag and wrap my arms around Linda. "Thank you so much . . . seriously . . . thank you."

Linda hugs me back and doesn't let go for a long time. "I still can't believe your grandparents are letting you do this drive."

"Neither can they," I say. "But my mom is my legal guardian, and she said it's okay."

"Well, I can't believe your mom is letting you go. I'd never let my daughter drive to Texas by herself."

"Sierra is only thirteen."

"Even when she's seventeen, she's not getting in a car and driving two thousand miles."

"I'll be eighteen in September."

"Well, then." Linda pauses. "Will you take good care of yourself?"

"Yeah."

"Does Sam know you're going?"

Terrence, our shift manager, bursts into the kitchen.

"Ladies!" he shouts. "Time for V's good-bye party!"

Linda links elbows with me, and we head out to the dining room, where the servers, the dishwashers, and three of our regular customers are standing around a long table filled with pan pizzas. I've spent the past four days working double shifts to save money for my drive, so I'm pizza-ed out. But I'm still touched by the party, especially since before today I never even realized these people cared if I showed up for work. As Terrence passes out soda, Russell sidles over to me.

"Want to hang out later? We could have a little good-bye party of our own."

I tell Russell I'm leaving first thing tomorrow and need to pack tonight.

"Attention, everyone!" Terrence shouts, whacking a fork against a hard plastic cup. "Let's all raise a glass for V."

Terrence makes a speech about how I've been a dedicated employee of Pizza Hut for almost a year and everyone is going to miss me. When he's done talking, he presents me with a Pizza Hut gift card.

"This baby is filled with enough cash for you to eat pizza at every intersection from here to Texas," Terrence says.

"Just what V wants," Linda murmurs.

One of the regulars gives me a book called *Let's Go USA*. The other dishwasher unscrews a jug of cheap wine. Terrence launches into a lecture about how he doesn't condone underage drinking and, if anyone asks, he didn't see it. Then he passes out another round of cups, and everyone starts making toasts and telling road-trip stories and asking me to send them postcards from Texas.

When I wake up the next morning, my car is gone.

I was planning to get up at eight and hit the road by nine, but I was up until two thirty in the morning, so when my alarm rang, I whacked it off and fell back asleep until ten. I hadn't meant to stay up so late, but I was peeling photos off the walls and riffling through piles of clothes, tossing things into a suitcase for my trip, debating whether or not to bring makeup and padded bras and sexy tops. They went in and they came out and, finally, they went in again.

Around midnight I called Chastity down in Florida to tell her I probably wouldn't be back until the end of the summer. Trinity grabbed the phone and started babbling about the party scene in Daytona Beach and how it makes Brockport look like the Vatican. I'd just hung up with the twins when Amos called. For a second I got a rush from hearing his voice. But as he began describing in intimate detail his camping trip and how he'd crossed rivers and fended off frostbite and caught trout, which he gutted and roasted over a bonfire, I remembered that Amos and I are only good when we're going at it.

As soon as I notice that my car is missing, I rush down the stairs. There's a note from my grandparents on the cutting board saying that they drove my car out to Albion for one more checkup and they'd be back by ten, eleven at the latest.

I crumple the paper in my fist. *Damn.* They know I got a tune-up last Thursday. They even offered to pay for it. I quickly call my grandpa's cell phone, but it goes straight to voice mail. Five minutes later he calls back with this big story about how Kent is the only mechanic he trusts and it's a good thing he brought my car in because they've discovered that my odometer has surpassed seventy thousand miles, which means the timing belt needs to be replaced and it's no small job, but Kent is making it his top priority, so they should be home by one, two at the latest.

After we hang up, I stomp around the house. What the hell is a timing belt anyway? I drop some frozen waffles into the toaster and then douse them with syrup. I drink a Dr Pepper. I leave a message with Aimee. I take the padded bras out of my suitcase and then tuck them back in again.

My grandparents don't get home until four thirty. By this time I have my luggage piled at the end of the driveway.

My grandpa pops the hood and points out the cover of the timing belt, as if the inner workings of a Volkswagen mean anything to me. Then he rambles on about valves and pistons and how if the timing belt slipped, it could cause serious engine damage, leaving me stranded on the roadside.

Once he's done I haul my suitcase into the trunk. I set my snacks on the passenger seat, along with my iPod, my phone, and my bag. I toss the wilderness supplies from my grandma into the backseat because she'd probably flip if I didn't bring along the compass or the pocketknife. As I'm leaning into the back, I notice that my strappy graduation sandals are still on the floor.

"Do you know where you're sleeping tonight?" my grandpa asks, staring down at my atlas.

"Probably Pennsylvania," I say. "It depends on how far I can make it before dark."

"Do you know how to get onto the thruway?"

"I take Nineteen through Bergen."

"Right," he says. "Head west, toward Buffalo."

"Buffalo," I repeat, tossing the atlas onto the backseat.

"That hockey puck you have on the dashboard," my grandma says. "Is it the one that hit you?"

I glance into my car. "Yeah . . . that's it."

"Have you told Sam you're going to Texas?" she asks.

I shake my head.

"Don't you think that's a good idea? He may stop by, and I'd hate for him to—"

"Sam's in California," I say.

"California?" my grandparents ask in unison.

I can see where this conversation is headed and I don't like it, so I quickly say, "Okay . . . well . . . I'm going to go."

They hug me really tight, and then I slide into my car and turn the key. I'm about to back down the driveway when my grandpa rushes to my window.

"We can still buy you a plane ticket," he says. "It's not too late to change your mind."

"Thanks," I say, honking twice and pressing my toe on the gas.

When I reach the end of Centennial, I take a right. I'm heading south on Route 19. In about nine seconds, I'll be passing the entrance to Sweden Village, where you turn to get to Sam's house. I consider doing a quick drive-by, but then I remind myself that's not why I'm going on this trip, so I accelerate through the light, up the hill, and out of town.

9

I glance at Brockport in my rearview mirror. I can't help but think about the day I arrived here. It was late afternoon, the middle of January, and the landscape was so barren. As my plane descended into Rochester, I stared at the graying snowdrifts and gnawed my nails and pictured Aimee frolicking on a tropical beach with some twenty-two-year-old surfer, downing piña coladas decorated with colorful paper umbrellas.

I could already tell it was going to be cold down there. Of course, I was only wearing jeans and a tank top because Aimee and I got into an argument on the cab ride to the San Diego Airport, where I was flying east and she was flying south. As I was checking in, I was so angry, I forgot to pull a sweatshirt out of my duffel bag. The flight attendants were bitches and wouldn't give me a blanket and I was hungry because they didn't have meal service and I forgot to bring anything to eat and the movie sucked and the guy next to me wouldn't stop humming and I scrounged up a pen, but I didn't have any paper, so I scrawled *fuck* onto all my fingers and *everyone* down my thumb.

I can still remember that fight with Aimee practically word for word. It started by me saying how she'd dragged me everywhere for sixteen years, so why dump me with my grandparents now? She kept insisting that the schools weren't great where she was going, as if she'd given a damn about my education before. She even ventured to say that this was best for all of us.

"Best?" I asked. "So you can have all the sex you want without worrying about anyone else?"

The cabdriver whistled under his breath.

"Watch yourself," Aimee hissed.

From there it lapsed into how I couldn't believe she'd cheated on Michael and I hadn't even gotten a chance to say good-bye to him and why couldn't we wait until he got back from that movie set in Vancouver? Also, whenever I asked Aimee how Michael had reacted when she told him, she just said, "I don't want to talk about it," which only made me madder because after all she'd put me through, at least I deserved more information.

I'm slowing at the train tracks in Bergen when it suddenly hits me. *I cheated on Sam just like Aimee cheated on Michael!* It's not like Sam and I were living together, and it's not like I ran off to Costa Rica with Amos — thank God — but it's not altogether different, either.

I've always imagined I'm the opposite of my mom, the way she moves in with her boyfriends and I prefer to keep my distance, but maybe I'm more like her than I thought. Or maybe Aimee had her reasons for leaving Michael and didn't want to burden me with them, and I basically told her she was a horrible person when I never stopped to think about it from her perspective, and maybe if I hadn't been so harsh, she would have taken me to Costa Rica with her.

I'm on the verge of feeling like complete crap when I tell myself, *Stop*. The Aimee-Michael thing was a year and a half ago. Now it's warm and breezy, and the early-evening sky is a perfect blue. There are wildflowers all over the roadside. My hair is in a loose ponytail. I'm blasting music, and the best part is that I spent an hour last night selecting 732 songs that won't remind me of Sam. I have a full tank of gas, a stash of snacks, and in less than a week, I'll be with Aimee in Texas and everything, or at least most things, will be better.

I was supposed to get on the thruway a few miles after Bergen, but as I approach the entrance, there's a blockade and a police officer is using her megaphone to wave cars along.

I slow down and lean out my window. "What's going on?"

"Accident on the thruway!" she calls through her megaphone. "Take Twenty instead!"

"Twenty?" I ask. I know I'm stalling traffic, but I can't reach my atlas in the back and I haven't exactly memorized the highway systems of western New York.

"Where're you headed?" the police officer asks.

"Texas," I say. When she gives me a funny look, I quickly add, "I'm going west."

"Stay south until you hit Twenty. Of course, that'd bring you near Darien Lake and it's gridlocked today, some big concert. So you could take Twenty A, or if you wanted to make better time, stay on Nineteen until you hit Eighty-six in the Southern Tier. Then again, Nineteen is slow, so you should probably do Three-ninety South for a while until—"

The silver pickup truck behind me starts honking, so the police officer lifts her megaphone again.

"Keep moving!" she shouts. Then she waves her arms in the direction of the entire southwestern United States. "Good luck!"

As I continue past the thruway ramp, I'm totally confused. Nineteen to 20? Nineteen to 20 A? Nineteen to the Southern Tier? I should pull over and glance at my map, except the silver pickup is on my butt and, judging by the driver's splotchy face in my rearview, I'm guessing he's skipped his anger-management class today. I gesture for him to pass, but he honks twice and sticks his middle finger out the window.

Oh, my God, I think, glancing at his thick plastic serial-killer glasses. *He's an escaped convict.* I know there's a federal prison around here, Attica or something. Just my luck. He tunneled out of his cell, hoisted a truck, and after twenty years in solitary confinement, I'm the first person to piss him off.

I press hard on the gas. I drive through Le Roy, past 20, past 20 A. I think the police officer said 86 is the fastest route, so I figure I'll look for that, maybe swing onto 390 on the way down. As I'm driving, I'm listening to music and watching the road and trying not to think about the pickup truck behind me. Finally, the escaped convict switches on his signal, flips me one more bird, and turns onto a smaller road.

I'm relieved to have dodged a violent bludgeoning, but then, up on the left, I spot a sign that says SWAIN MOUNTAIN with a little picture of a downhill skier.

Oh, no. Total Sam flashback.

In early April, about a month after Sam and I started hanging out, he invited me to come to Swain with him and Luca. It was the last weekend the lifts were running, and even though the snow was slushy, he convinced me it was going to be great. Sam and Luca brought their snowboards. I'd never been on a slope before, so Sam suggested I rent skis instead because they're easier for stopping. I remember thinking how my father was supposedly this champion downhill skier, so maybe I inherited some skills from him.

I totally didn't. As Luca hopped on the lift to the black diamonds, Sam led me to a bunny hill and showed me how to snap my boots into my bindings and explained about snowplowing and told me how, if I felt out of control, I should sit down. He held onto my hips as I inched sideways up the incline, but then as soon as he let go, I toppled over, twisted my knee, and smacked my head on the ice.

"I suck," I moaned.

"It's okay," Sam said, wiping the snow off my cheek with his gloved hand. "It happens to everyone."

After my fifteenth nosedive, Sam conceded that it seemed to be happening more to me than most people.

"Why don't we take a break?" he asked. "We can try again later."

I urged Sam to find Luca and do some snowboarding, but he insisted on coming into the lodge and buying us hot chocolates and nachos. We found a table off to one side, and we were being all cuddly, kissing and feeding each other cheese-drenched chips. As I stood up and clomped toward the bathroom, Sam took my picture with his phone. "To commemorate your illustrious stint as a skier," he said, laughing.

"Ha," I said.

I went to the bathroom and then bought some water. As I was clomping back to the table, I noticed that Luca had joined Sam. Their backs were to me, but I could see they were looking at the picture on Sam's phone.

". . . but it still sucks about today," I heard Luca say.

"I don't mind," Sam said. "I mean, she's worth it."

"Flaws and all?" Luca asked.

"I like the flaws best," Sam said. "They make her real."

I remember standing there in my damp jeans and those heavy ski boots, thinking how that was the nicest thing anyone had ever said about me.

Okay, I'll admit it, I don't know where the hell I am. It's getting dark and I'm surrounded by hulking hills and I know I had everyone convinced I'm this experienced driver, but the truth is that when I went to Syracuse for a show last December, I smoked too much weed in the parking lot and this other kid had to drive my car home.

Plus, I just saw this warning sign about black bears, so every time I spot a tree, I think it's an animal and I swerve into oncoming traffic. Luckily, there's no oncoming traffic. That's the upside of wandering this web of unmarked roads with barely any shoulder to pull onto and look at my map. Even if I did, I'm so lost, I'd have no idea where to begin. Also, there's the black-bear factor. It's not like *they* have signs saying, PLEASE DON'T ATTACK THE PEOPLE.

I think I got lost somewhere near Swain. I was distracted thinking about Sam and took a left instead of going straight and then—

Shit!

I see what appears to be a bear on the side of the road and jerk the wheel, but this time there's a pair of headlights coming toward me. The other car honks, swerves hard onto the gravel, and then continues by. I keep driving, too, but my heart is racing and I'm biting so hard on my lower lip, I think I can taste blood.

I pull out my phone to call Aimee or Mara or even the twins, just to hear a familiar voice. Of course, there's no cell-phone reception, which means if I get mutilated by a bear, I can't even dial for help.

I see a motel coming up, so I slow down a little. There aren't any cars out front, but I notice a faint light at the far end, near a sign labeled OFFICE. I steer into the parking lot, scan for bears, and then hurry through the door.

I step inside a small room that reeks of stale cigars. It's covered floor to ceiling in dusty bundles of newspapers, and there's an ancient guy hunched over a scratched desk, so motionless that for a second I wonder if he's dead. But then he pushes his glasses down his fleshy nose and growls, "Whaddya want?"

I chew on my thumbnail. "Uhhh . . . a room?"

He scrounges around in a drawer, tosses me a rusty key, and barks, "Room seven."

Then he shoves his glasses up on his nose and goes back to his newspaper.

"Don't you want me to pay?" I ask.

"You planning to run off?"

"No."

"Well, then."

"Can I ask you . . ." I pause. "Could you tell me where we are? I got a little lost on my way to Buffalo."

"From where?"

"Brockport."

He stares up at me, his eyes milky with cataracts, and then launches into this phlegmy laugh. "Honey, you're in Steuben County."

"Where?"

"Southern Tier, near the Pennsylvania border," he says. "You sure did get lost."

I rush down the dark walkway until I reach a door labeled 7. I fit the key into the lock, turn the knob, and reach for a switch.

Nothing.

I hesitate for a second before fumbling along the wall until I get to the bathroom, where I find a functioning light.

I turn and look around. There's a lopsided bed, a wobbly nightstand, and a small table sagging under the weight of the television. I attempt to turn on the lamp next to the bed, but it doesn't work. I hurry over and close the front door. As I'm rotating the lock, I can't help but notice that it's just a dinky sliver of metal, easily kick-through-able, if someone were so inclined.

I sit on the edge of the bed. It's so quiet my ears are ringing. As I run my palms over my knees, I suddenly remember that, oh yeah, I hate being alone. No, I don't just hate it. It freaks me out. My brain starts racing fast while the rest of my body is moving in slow motion. It's scary, almost like I can't control my thoughts.

I cross the dark room and press the power button on the television. Of course, it doesn't work, so I dig in my bag for my headphones, but then I remember that I left my iPod in the car. I check my phone one more time. Still no reception. My breath is coming in short, panicky gasps. I collapse on the bedspread, press my hands over my eyes, and wish for all of this to be over.

10

I have to pee all night, but I'm refusing to walk to the bathroom because I keep hearing little mice toenails scurrying around the floor. And that's not the worst part. Neither is this sorrowful moaning coming from outside my door. It started around midnight and has been going constantly for hours. And that's not even the worst part. Neither is the fact that I'm die-of-frostbite cold. Of course, I'm only wearing a tank top and a skirt, but there's no way in hell I'm going to my car to get warm clothes and there's less of a way in hell I'm pulling back this bedspread and crawling into the mouse droppings that are most likely lurking underneath.

The worst part is that I'm completely alone.

All night I feel like I'm hovering outside my body. I'm looking down and watching myself lying there, my hair splayed on the pillow, my hands over my eyes, and I keep thinking, *This is why I chase guys. This is why I do the plays. This is why I go to parties.* Because then I never have to be in a situation like this, crumpled on a motel bed with nothing but my pathetic self to keep me company.

"So you're the girl who got lost on her way to Buffalo?" the woman in the office asks.

"Yeah."

She chuckles. "You really left from Brockport?"

"Yep."

"Do you realize you drove more than a hundred miles in the wrong direction?"

"I guess."

It's ten thirty in the morning. Sometime around dawn, the moaning stopped and the mice took a break and I dashed to the bathroom. I peed, grabbed a towel to wrap around my icy feet, and then collapsed onto the bed. When I woke up a few hours later, I gathered my hair into a ponytail, washed my face in the rust-hued water, and shoved my phone into my bag. As I stepped into the office, there was a woman at the desk. She had thinning hair and a big brown mole on her cheek. Actually, calling it a mole trivializes the whole thing. It's more like a continent.

She chuckles some more, but when she notices I'm not smiling along with her, she tells me how much I owe for the night. I hand her some cash and ask if she can help me get to the thruway.

"Where to now?" she asks. "London? Paris?"

I calmly explain that I'm going to Texas to see my mom and need to figure out how to get to I-90. She studies my face for a long moment and then rips a piece of paper out of a notebook and draws me a map. She labels all the lefts and rights that will lead to the Southern Tier Expressway. Once I get on that I can cruise to Erie, where I'll finally pick up 90.

As I'm heading toward the door, she calls out, "I just have to say . . . I've been working here for thirty-three years, and I've never heard of anyone getting that lost."

"You have no idea," I mutter before walking to my car.

As I'm pulling out of the motel, I consider glancing at that compass from my grandma, just to make sure I'm headed in the right direction. But then I think how proud it would make her, so I switch on my blinker and wing it instead.

I find the expressway no problem. Right before the entrance ramp, I stop at a gas station and fill my tank. I end up splashing gasoline all over my fingers, which, of course, reminds me of Sam because there was this one night we drove into Gates to see a movie, and on the way, he got gas on his hand and I joked that I wouldn't share a popcorn with him, which I totally did anyway.

I hurry into the bathroom and scrub with soap, but the smell lingers. As I'm buying a cup of coffee and a box of brown sugar Pop-Tarts, I ask the woman at the cash register if she has any suggestions for getting gasoline off my skin, but she just stares blankly out the window.

An hour later, as I'm cruising down the highway, I'm still feeling awful. Every vehicle on this road is an SUV jam-packed with a family. It's the Great American Road Trip, sing-along bonding, license-plate counting, twenty national monuments in ten days. To be perfectly honest, it makes me want to scream.

I never told Sam this, but it used to drive me crazy when we'd be hanging out at his house and his parents would swarm in and Rachel would join us and someone would produce a plate of snickerdoodles and they'd all start reminiscing about their trip to Japan and then they'd lapse into some memory from nine years ago and then, invariably, Sam's mom would open her scrapbooks or Sam's dad would put on a home movie and Sam and Rachel would groan, but you could tell they were loving it.

Maybe I wouldn't hate families so much if I knew more about my dad. I'm not that stereotypical fatherless child who spends weeks and months imagining her dad is some rich guy who will come rescue her and then they'll ride off together into the sunset. But I just wish I had a little more information, like maybe it'd help crack some code about what makes me operate. Aimee has said I have his nose, but I have to imagine there's more.

Also, even though it's sunny and blue, I still haven't gotten over last night. That silence in my ears. The scary way my brain was racing. And especially the horrible sense that when I don't have anyone around to acknowledge my presence, I don't actually exist.

I'm driving along the northern rim of Allegany State Park when I pull out the number of Linda's cousin from Erie. I wasn't planning to take Linda up on her offer, but I'm starting to feel this urgent need to have immediate contact with another human being.

"Hello?" a man's voice asks.

"My name is V," I say. "I used to work with Linda Anderson at Pizza Hut, and I'm driving to Texas and I—"

"Well, hello! This is Linda's cousin Darren. We were hoping to hear from you. Are you going to be stopping by?"

I tell him I'm on the Southern Tier Expressway, heading toward Erie. He insists I sleep over at their house tonight. He tells me that he and his wife are about to leave for a concert in Chautauqua and won't be home until later, but his son will be around and maybe even his daughter.

"Let me give you directions to the house," Darren says.

I can hear a woman's voice in the background.

"Hold on . . . my wife says we're too hard to find . . . we're all the way out on the lake . . . hold on a minute."

After much conferring and what sounds like a hurried telephone exchange, Darren tells me that when I get to Erie, I should go to this place called Café Diem. He gives me the directions and tells me it has an orange flag with a bright yellow sunshine out front. His son, Nate, is working at the nearby mall, and he'll meet me there when he gets off at three. After that I can follow him to their house.

"Do you have a pen?" he asks. "I'll give you Nate's cell phone, just in case."

I rummage through my glove compartment. As he recites the number, I scribble everything onto the back of my hand.

"And you have the address of the café?"

"Peach Street," I say. "On the left, across from the hospital."

"It has an orange flag with a sunshine."

"Got it."

I make it to Café Diem by two thirty, so I order an iced mocha and settle into a table near the windows. I'm just reaching for my phone when Aimee calls.

"Hey!" she says. "Where are you?"

"Erie, Pennsylvania," I say. "And that's so funny because I was about to call you."

"Erie? Didn't you leave yesterday?"

I tell her how I didn't leave until really late and then I got lost and ended up in some motel in Steuben County and it was filthy and gross and, in all our moves, Aimee never made us stay anywhere that awful.

"Of course we did," Aimee says. "You were probably too young to remember."

"Well, I bet it wasn't this bad."

"Honey, you're doing great. You're trying, right? That's more than most people can say."

I sip some mocha. "May I ask you a huge question?"

"How huge?"

"Well . . . you've told me that you never knew my father's last name, and I—"

"The Sperm Donor?" Aimee asks. "That's huge."

"I was just wondering . . . do you know his last name after all and you were trying to protect me?"

"Oh, V," Aimee says, sighing.

"What?"

"I wish I knew more. I was so young and, honestly, I didn't know better. His name was Brian and he was a ski instructor, but I was at Vail and he was over in Aspen. I only saw him a few times. He was Irish . . . I know that. He had an Irish last name."

"Like what? There are a lot of Irish last names."

"God, I'm so sorry. . . ." Aimee is quiet for a moment. "Tell you what. I'll try to remember everything I can, and when you get to San Antonio, we'll talk all about it."

I exhale softly and then say, "That sounds good."

As soon as we hang up, the door jingles and this guy walks in. His jeans and shirt are dusty, but it's obvious that he's hot. And built. *Seriously* built.

As he scans the café, I wonder whether this is Linda's cousin's son. Linda is black, so I'm assuming her cousin is black. This guy looks multiracial, like part black and part white or maybe part Asian. When his dad said he worked at the mall, I imagined Taco Bell or the Gap. I didn't picture construction. I definitely didn't picture all those muscles.

If I were in any other head space, I'd be pouncing all over this guy, working it hard. But right now . . . I don't know. I just don't feel like myself these days.

You have to try, V. This is why you're here, to forget about Brockport, to reclaim some of who you used to be.

I grab my phone and dial the number on my hand.

"Hello?" he asks, lifting his phone to his ear.

So it *is* Nate.

"You know," I say, chewing on the tip of my straw. "Your dad didn't tell me you were hot."

He quickly looks around. When he sees me by the windows, he grins and says, "Maybe my dad doesn't think I'm hot."

I smile back at him. As he walks toward me, I start wondering whether maybe this won't be so hard, after all.

11

It takes me six minutes to realize that Nate Anderson is going to be the perfect remedy for getting over Sam. When he joins my table, he swigs his bottle of water and tells me how he's doing a construction job at the mall, tearing up parking lots and putting in new ones. Or at least it's something like that. As he talks, he keeps getting texts on his phone. He reads them, dashes quick responses, and then looks up at me and goes, "So what were you saying?"

"You were telling me about parking lots."

And he launches back into the details of the decimation process, but then his phone vibrates and he glances down, and then, a moment later, he's asking what I was saying again.

Nate's attention-deficit problem is perfect. Even though Sam would sometimes call and text people, he never let it take priority over our time together. But when a guy spends half his time pecking away at his phone, you just know it's not going to get too serious.

Nate's day job doesn't hurt things, either. I swear, his biceps look like he's been ripping out those slabs of concrete with his bare hands.

"So that's what you do?" I ask as Nate finishes replying to his latest message.

"You mean construction?"

"Yeah."

"Just for the summer." Nate chugs some more water. "I go to Ohio State. . . . I'm studying athletic training."

"What's that?"

As Nate describes how he'll be the guy who runs onto the field when a professional athlete gets injured, I'm about to point out the scar on my forehead. But then his phone vibrates, which is a good thing, because if I told him about the hockey puck, the conversation might have strayed to Sam. So instead, I watch Nate and I think, *athletic training . . . so jocky . . . so physical . . . so different from Sam.* Sam was going to study history and political science. Sam would rather spend Super Bowl Sunday in the library, reading about an obscure uprising two hundred years ago in some country that no longer exists.

"What were you saying?" Nate asks, looking up at me.

I smile. "You were telling me about athletic training."

As I said, the perfect breakup remedy.

*   *   *

I follow Nate's Jeep onto the highway, off the highway, around corners, through intersections, and down an unmarked dirt road. I consider calling his phone and asking whether he's single, just to see if this even harbors a possibility, but he's driving so fast, it's all I can do just to keep up.

We pull into the driveway and cut our engines. Actually, it's more of a gravelly loop. Beyond that, there's a ranch house with a grassy lawn that slopes down to the waterfront, complete with a dock and a speedboat.

I pull down my visor and glance into the mirror. *Not bad,* I think, yanking my hair out of its ponytail. Especially since I didn't shower this morning and I have on the same clothes from yesterday. Of course, I didn't realize Linda's cousin's son was going to be hot, so I'm not wearing any makeup and my legs are stubbly. At this point I just need to find a bathroom and shave and change into something cuter, maybe my navy halter dress with the strapless push-up bra. I actually packed the super-sexy dress I bought for graduation, but that'd give the impression I'm trying too hard, and if I can wrangle Nate away from his phone, I should probably make him work a little.

I comb my fingers through my hair, slide on some lip gloss, and meander toward Nate's Jeep. He's still in the seat, gathering stuff into an athletic bag.

"That person you were texting," I call through the open window, "is she your girlfriend?"

Nate turns off his music and joins me on the driveway. "Why do you ask?"

I grin. "I'm taking that as a no."

"Since you're wondering . . . let's just say there's no one person right now."

"Now we're talking definite no," I say, laughing.

Nate studies me for a moment. "So what do you want to do?" he asks. "You're staying overnight, right? Want to take out the boat and go waterskiing? I think my sister's around. We could probably get her to spot."

I glance at the dock. I've never been waterskiing before, but if my downhill ability is any indicator, I should probably avoid that sport, too. Also, after my run-in with Rachel, I'm not in the mood to involve anyone's sister in my romantic pursuits.

"Maybe we can just hang out at the dock?" I ask.

"Sure . . . I usually go swimming after work."

"Is it cold?"

"Yeah. It's freezing this year."

I tell Nate how I still haven't thawed from my motel room last night, and, speaking of, maybe he can lead me to a place where I can shower. Nate nods and then strolls toward my car. He opens the driver's-side door, pops the trunk, and asks what he can carry up to the guest room. He's all take-charge about it, which I know should make me feel girly and grateful, but I can't help wondering whether Sam would carry my bags or whether he'd say something like *I know you're strong and can*—

STOP!

I need to stop thinking about Sam.

And, honestly, the best way to stop thinking about Sam is to see Nate in as little clothes as possible as soon as possible.

As I'm lounging on the dock, watching Nate's orgasmic body plunge in and out of Lake Erie, I'm still thinking about Sam. It's the same thing in the kitchen later. Nate has a towel wrapped around his waist and his sister, Delia, is eating a peach at the breakfast nook and I'm sitting on a stool, drinking a Coke and chiming in with the occasional commentary. I can tell by the way Nate is laughing at my every word that my navy halter and push-up bra are totally doing the trick. If I had any doubt, though, as soon as Delia leaves to see her boyfriend for the evening, Nate twists up his towel and snaps it toward my butt, which should have sent me into throes of ecstasy, right?

Wrong.

I am still, pathetically, thinking about Sam.

Partially, I'm wondering what he'd say if he knew I was in Pennsylvania with some guy. But also, no matter how gorgeous and emotionally unavailable Nate is, there's this part of me that wishes Sam were here instead. I can imagine him making me dinner, and then, once it got dark, we'd skinny-dip in the lake and sprint naked across the lawn and tumble into that king-size guest bed and fool around for hours.

But Sam is not here and, worse, he's all the way in

California, so I tilt my head to one side and say, "Don't you know that if you swat a girl's butt, she's going to think you're into her?"

Nate smiles. "Is that what you want to think?"

"You didn't answer my question. Should I send you a text and ask you instead?"

Nate snaps the towel toward me again, this time grazing my thigh.

"Okay," I say, sipping some Coke. "I'm taking that as a yes."

Nate wraps the towel around his waist. "Do you like hot dogs?"

When he says that, I laugh so hard I spew my soda across the kitchen.

"You," Nate says, tickling my waist, "have a seriously twisted mind."

I'm still choking when Nate heads outside and shakes a bag of charcoal into the grill.

I guess things get better out on the deck. Nate barbecues hot dogs and I laze in the hammock and we have a beer and then, when he comes out with the buns, he tosses me another beer, which I drink faster than the first. By the time we sit down at the picnic table, I'm pretty buzzed and, I have to admit, I like the way he's looking at me. Also, when his phone vibrates over on the banister, he doesn't even get up to check it.

As Nate dumps our plates into the trash, he says, "So what do you want to do now? I could call some buddies and—"

"How about we go into your room and look at your coin collection?" I ask.

"I don't have a coin collection."

"Exactly."

Nate grins at me and then leads the way back into the house. As soon as we get to his room, we start kissing. After a while he unties my halter and I unhook my bra and, before long, we're rolling around his bed. Nate has wriggled off his shorts, and I can feel through his boxers that he's hard. He pushes up my dress and circles his fingers around my belly, slowly inching lower and lower. I know I should be turned on, but I'm totally not. I move his hand away from me, reach through the opening of his boxers, and, basically, take the necessary steps to finish things off.

A few minutes later, Nate falls asleep. I rehook my bra, tie my dress around my shoulders, and tiptoe out of the room.

Sam and I waited a month before we had sex.

That's what I think as I rock in the Andersons' hammock and stare up at the sky. I came out to the deck because I was lying in the guest bed and I felt like I couldn't breathe, so I thought some fresh air might help. But I've been here for over an hour. I saw Nate's parents pull up to the house. I saw the lights come on and go off again. I saw the stars disappear behind murky clouds. And I still can't breathe. And I still can't stop thinking about Sam.

He was a virgin when we met. He'd fooled around with several girls, but he told me from the start that he put sex in a different category, something you do when you actually care about the other person.

I, on the other hand, lost my virginity when I was fourteen. It was with a guy in Vermont, when Aimee and I lived on an artists' commune. He was eighteen and cute in a sensitive-but-clinically-depressed kind of way. We did it one Saturday night when Aimee was working late and I invited him over to keep me company. I'd taken a bus to the mall earlier that day, blew some cash at Victoria's Secret, bought condoms, and then spent the rest of the afternoon plotting how to get him into bed. When we actually did it, we were tangled on the couch and both of us still had our jeans on, just pushed down in key regions, and, honestly, there was nothing pleasurable about getting a dick forced into a place that could barely accommodate a tampon. We did it a few more times that week, and it definitely started hurting less, but by that point we were both sick of each other.

I had more meaningless hookups in New Orleans, which is where we moved after Vermont, and Oregon, which is where we moved after New Orleans, and San Diego, which is where we moved after Oregon. During my first year in Brockport, I slept with two guys and had flings with six or seven others. I guess I didn't see sex as a big deal. It was just something you do when you're young, like smoking weed in graveyards and drinking forties from brown paper bags.

From the start, everything with Sam was different. It took us forever to kiss. I think it was at least a week because I'd just gotten my stitches out and he came over to see how I was doing and we were sitting on my bed and chatting and the sexual tension was seriously high. When our lips finally touched, it was so intense I remember thinking, *So THIS is what the big deal is about.*

That's all we did those next few weeks. We made out until my mouth was numb and my cheeks were flushed and my underwear was wet. And, finally, on a windy weekend in April, Sam's parents took Rachel on a college tour. Sam invited me over, and we went straight up to his bedroom and slowly removed every article of each other's clothing. Sam noticed my hands were trembling, and he kissed each of my fingers, one by one, before rolling on a condom and sliding inside of me. As he did, I remember getting a feeling in my stomach that this was the most important moment in my entire life.

Of course, we didn't always have so much blissful solitude. Sometimes it was a quick fix before my grandparents got home. Sometimes it was a stealthy squeeze, blasting music in his room and telling his mom we were doing our homework. But, even so, it never stopped feeling like a big deal. And, unlike with every other guy, I never wanted to run away as soon as it was over.

12

The good news is that by the time I wake up, Nate is already decimating a parking lot. The bad news is that as I wander into the kitchen in search of caffeine, Nate's parents are sitting at the breakfast table. Nate's dad is staring at a laptop. Nate's mom is flipping through the newspaper. As soon as they see me, they both smile.

"You must be V!" his dad exclaims.

"We're so sorry we missed you yesterday," his mom says.

His dad is in his mid-fifties, with smooth skin and a small hoop in his ear. His mom is a sporty-looking Asian woman, her hair cinched into a ponytail, her spotless sneakers raring to hit the tennis courts.

"Well," Nate's dad says, "Nate certainly enjoyed spending time with you."

"And now we get to," his mom says.

"So tell us all about yourself," his dad says.

"How long have you worked with Linda?" his mom asks.

"Have you met Sierra?" his dad asks. "Isn't she the sweetest thing?"

I'm standing in the doorway, completely paralyzed. I'm not the biggest fan of parents, especially the high-energy types who want to be your new best friend. Also, when you've just had intimate contact with their son's penis, it's hard to bounce into casual chitchat over orange juice and a sesame bagel.

I can hear my phone ringing in the guest room. I dash down the hallway and grab it off the bed. It just turns out to be my grandparents. This must be their tenth call since I left Brockport. I clench my jaw as they explain how they've been following the weather patterns across northern Ohio and it looks like there are severe thunderstorms coming and maybe I should stay with Linda's cousins for an extra night.

I tell them I'll think about it. But then, as soon as we hang up, my low-battery signal bleeps, and instead of plugging in my phone and sticking around while it recharges, I shove it into my bag, strip the bed, and straighten the pillows. Then I head into the kitchen, where I thank Nate's parents for letting me sleep over and say how I need to clock some good mileage before the storm hits.

The rain starts about twenty minutes into my drive. At first it's not bad. But by the time I cross the border into Ohio, it's pelting down so hard, I can barely see. Even though my windshield wipers are on high, they're just smearing the water from side to side. I grip the wheel and attempt to navigate between the lines, but every few minutes a truck cuts me off, sending me lurching over the shoulder. My heart collides with my rib cage, and I swear I'm going to crash and my car will crumple like a paper bag and I'll die instantly.

It doesn't help that I have a caffeine-deprivation headache. And I've barely slept the past two nights, so I'm completely zonked. And when I reach for my phone to call Mara, I discover the battery is dead. And my gas gauge says I have less than a quarter tank, but the storm is so bad I'm scared to pull over and fuel up.

To make matters worse, I can't stop obsessing about how I lured Nate into his bed. Did I really think some stupid hand job was going to make everything better?

A truck veers in front of me, drenching my windshield with water. For a moment I'm blinded. I grip my wheel and think, *This is it. . . . I'm going to die.* But then I can see again, and although I haven't crashed, I've somehow steered into the express lane and there's so much traffic I can't get back across. The sky is an angry purple and thunder is booming and signs are indicating some direction I don't think I want to be going and one song ends and another comes on and—

Oh no.

It's Sam's song, that ballad about two people who are total soul mates and miss each other when they can't be together. Sam listened to it constantly. It was even playing when we had that fight in his backyard after graduation.

Damn.

How did I not take this off my iPod?

Damn. Damn. Damn.

The tears are streaming down my cheeks, and I must have swerved again because this other car is honking at me. There's a wide shoulder coming up. I tap my brake and ease onto the side of the road. As soon as I shift into park, I collapse into sobs.

Oh, my God.

I have totally been in denial.

Sam and I were together.

Sam and I were *completely* together. No, not just together. We were in love, like Sam tried to tell me, only I pressed my hands over my ears and demanded that he never say those words in my presence again.

Oh, my God.

I bury my head in my hands and think about how I pushed Sam away and cheated on him and how I'm the most horrible person in the history of the universe.

When I finally look up, Demon Puck is staring at me. I arch into the backseat and paw through the bag from my grandma until I find that pocketknife. I flip out the largest blade and force it between Demon Puck and the dashboard. The puck snaps off and topples to the floor. I scoop it up, roll down the window, and chuck it into the muddy grass.

I thought that would be all cathartic, but when I close the window, I don't feel the slightest bit better. I rest my head on the steering wheel and start sobbing all over again.

When I wake up in the morning, I smell cigarettes and peppermint gum. I have no idea where I am. But then I stumble out of bed and part the heavy green curtains and stare at the strip malls and shopping centers, and I remember . . . oh yeah . . . melting down on the highway . . . coasting on fumes to a nearby motel . . . trudging through the rain into the lobby . . . being informed by the desk clerk that I was ten miles east of Cleveland . . . sleeping all afternoon . . . eating vending-machine crap for dinner . . . blasting the TV . . . and then fending off another night of unbearable silence.

At least it's not raining. That's what I think as I drive across Ohio. At least it's not raining because, other than that, my heart is heavy and I can't shake the feeling that I'm a terrible person and, no matter what, my mind keeps wandering back to Sam. I've decided that, partially, I was scared of him getting to know the real me. I mean, if I really let my guard down, that would require talking about my mom, and to talk about my mom is to admit that she doesn't love me—or maybe she does, but it's in this screwed-up way, and the only thing I've ever been able to interpret from that is that, deep down, I'm not worth loving. Which brings me back to my initial thought, that I could never let Sam get to know the real me because, eventually, he'd discover the same thing.

I'm curious to hear what Mara is going to say about this. I called her this morning when I stopped for gas and coffee. It's 350 miles from Cleveland to Chicago, so I told her I'd probably make it sometime in the evening. She said she's living near the University of Chicago, so I should get off at the Fifty-fifth Street exit, head east, and try her cell phone.

The best thing about Mara is that she tells it like it is. If I explain everything that happened with Sam and she agrees I was an asshole, she won't be afraid to say it. And, honestly, I'd probably benefit from someone saying it to my face, really letting me have it.

As I cross into Indiana, the landscape is mostly flat, with endless cornfields, and factories burping pollution into the thick, white sky. I see a service plaza coming up with a sign for McDonald's, and I suddenly realize I haven't eaten much since those two hot dogs in Erie.

I pull into the parking lot, grab my cash, and step outside. The air smells like freshly cut grass, and it's so humid my tank top is sticking to my stomach. I head into the bathroom, splash my face with water, and then study my reflection in the mirror for a long time.

A few minutes later, as I'm reading the overhead menu, the guy behind the counter says, "What do you want?"

I stare at him.

"What do you want?" he asks again.

What do I want?

I want to forget. If I can't forget, I want none of this to have happened. I want to have been born to a different mom or maybe she could have been older than nineteen and maybe she could have known my dad's last name and, maybe, that time we lived in Maine for twelve days, she would have listened when I told her how this girl in school invited me to a sleepover and we would have stayed in town after all and I would have gone to that party and made a huge group of friends and we would have remained close through high school and danced together at the prom and inscribed one another's yearbooks with things like "Let's be in touch forever" and actually have meant it.

But instead I mutter, "Chicken nuggets, fries, and a Coke."

As I hand him my money, I notice he's wearing a chunky silver ring that says CLUE. I wonder if that's a sign. Well, even if it is, it can't help me because I definitely don't have one.

13

As we're hauling my bags up the four flights of stairs to Mara's apartment, she tells me she's planned a Power Day for us tomorrow, complete with a tour of Chicago and several rounds of coffee.

"Ugh," I mutter, pausing on a landing.

"Not feeling powerful?" Mara turns to grin at me. "Or have you quit coffee? Please don't tell me you've quit coffee, because I can't be the only caffeine addict in the family."

"Aimee still drinks coffee," I say. But then, as we resume our ascent, I add, "At least I think so."

Mara opens the door and gestures me inside. We toss my stuff on the floor and I glance around. It's a crappy student apartment that Mara and her Yale roommate are subletting for the summer. Mara is a neat freak, so the living room is tidy. But all the cleaning products in the world couldn't disguise those yellowy stains on the futon or the unmistakable frat-boy stench of farts, beer, and late-night Chinese food.

"My room is on the left," Mara says. "You'll acquire the fewest diseases in there. Over there is Emmy's room. She's out all the time, so you probably won't see her, but don't be surprised if you hear sadomasochistic sex in the middle of the night."

"*Emmy?*" I ask, staring at Mara. My only memory of Emmy was when my grandparents and I visited Yale for Parents' Weekend and she was all equestrian team and pink cashmere sweater sets.

"I know," Mara says, rolling her eyes. "She's a different person since we got here. She met some guy, a graffiti artist. Luckily, they usually bring the handcuffs to his place."

"What about you?" I ask as Mara leads me into the kitchen and sets a bag of chips and a jar of salsa on the table.

"Handcuffs?" Mara shakes her head. "Nah . . . I prefer whips, sometimes blindfolds."

Mara laughs, and as she does, I laugh, too. It's great to finally see Mara. I can tell it's already been a good summer for her. Even she admits that she tends to go overboard with stressing about academics and her future as the CEO of a Fortune 500 company. So after an intense year at college, Mara decided to join her roommate in Chicago. Emmy is completing some premed requirements. Mara, on the other hand, is working at Starbucks and doing yoga and taking a drawing class. Plus, she's growing out her hair, so it's curly around her face. And she's wearing low-rise shorts and a white tank top that shows off her tanned shoulders.

After a moment I say, "You're avoiding my question."

Mara pours us glasses of water and indicates that I should sit down.

"Still avoiding," I say.

"Fine." Mara opens the chips and scoops out a handful. "There's a cute guy in my yoga class, but I have no idea how to ask if he wants to hang out. I haven't been with anyone since . . . well . . . since . . ."

"James?"

"Yeah," Mara says, grimacing.

James was Mara's boyfriend from Brockport. They worked at Common Grounds together during her senior year and were inseparable all of last summer. But then when she came home for Thanksgiving, they had a big talk and decided long-distance wasn't working for them. Mara told me it was a smart decision, but as she boarded the train back to New Haven, her eyes were puffy and bloodshot.

"So," Mara says, "any brilliant seduction advice? All I've done so far is ask how he does the camel pose so well."

"The camel pose?"

"Sort of like a back bend, but much more painful."

"You asked him how he does the *camel pose*?" I ask, grinning.

"I know!" Mara buries her face in her hands. "I'm pathetic."

I drag a chip through the salsa. "I can't get over the fact that you're taking yoga."

"Don't get me wrong. I still run to class all caffeinated and checking my voice mail." Mara sips her water. "But enough me about me. . . . How's the road trip going?"

I groan. "Can we please talk about Camel Guy instead?"

"Now look who's avoiding."

"Fine," I say, and then I describe driving one hundred miles in the wrong direction, fooling around with Nate in Erie, thinking I was going to crash in Cleveland, and then today how I trucked across Ohio and Indiana, but then hit construction before Gary and a standstill on the Skyway into Chicago. Also, I couldn't remember Mara's exit, and the bumper-car traffic was too terrifying for me to look away from the road and find my phone. By the time I finally called her, I had a pounding headache and I'd gnawed off all my fingernails.

"Why are you doing this again?" Mara asks. "Why not just fly out there? And speaking of Texas, why are you even going in the first place?"

I shake my head and tell Mara that I truly, deeply want to discuss the guy from her yoga class.

"Still avoiding," Mara says.

I yawn and rub my eyes.

"Now you're using the tired defense," Mara says. "But

I'll take it, seeing that you've just driven ten million miles. How about to-be-continued?"

I shrug. Mara puts the salsa in the fridge. Then we head down the hall and into her room. There's a twin bed, a desk with a laptop and some sketch pads, and a rectangle of available carpet space. Mara offers me the bed, but I tell her I'll crash on the floor.

"Do you have a sleeping bag?" she asks.

"It's in the car. Your parents—"

"Oh, my God! Did they buy you that zero-degree one from Dick's?"

"How'd you know?"

"They got one like that for me, too," she says. "Are they obsessed with the North Pole or something?"

"It actually looks okay . . . sort of cozy."

I reach into my pocket, but Mara takes the car keys out of my hand and insists on getting it herself. Once she's gone I collapse onto her bed and stare out the window. I can see the flickering blue of a neighbor's television. A car alarm begins shrieking and then stops. A commuter train whizzes by. I close my eyes and wait for Mara to get back.

Mara and I sleep until ten, shower, and then traipse down the four flights of stairs and onto the street. She's skipping her art class this morning and has announced that our Power Day will begin with a trek over to her Starbucks.

She's on an equally tight budget, but she said that if this one psychotic manager isn't around, we can probably score free lattes and maybe even some Danishes. Otherwise, we'll just use her employee discount for breakfast.

We turn right on Cornell and wander the quiet sidewalks of Hyde Park. The trees are lush and full. The brick row houses have trimmed lawns and wrought-iron fences. Mara tells me it's mostly a college neighborhood, which makes sense because we've passed a few tweedy professor types pedaling bicycles and some wan students lugging overstuffed backpacks.

After about ten minutes, we reach a populated strip with restaurants and bookstores. Mara steers me into Starbucks and introduces me to this skinny Indian guy named Navneet. He propels us behind a display of organic beans, leans in, and whispers, "Noelle just went to the pharmacy to pick up her Prozac. You want two drip coffees? I can do that quickly. With steamed milk? Okay? Okay."

Ninety seconds later Navneet chucks us a bulging bag. "I put in sugar packets and stirrers and napkins and a few apple streusels," he hisses. "Now get out of here!"

We thank him, and as we're saying good-bye, he smiles extra-long at Mara, and in that extra-long moment, I realize that if he ate seventy thousand apple streusels, he'd actually be cute. Also, he obviously has a thing for Mara, only she has no idea, or if she does, she's not letting on.

We hurry out the door, turn left, and cross the street to

a small park. We're just settling onto a bench when Mara hands me a coffee and says, "So now can you tell me why you're doing this road trip?"

I pry the lid off my cup. "What do you want to know?"

"All I know at this point is that things were over with Sam, and my parents were threatening to send you to therapy, and then you called and asked if you could stay here on your way to Texas. I assumed you were running away from Sam, but then you told me he's in California, so I'm confused."

"I guess I'm still running away," I say, "but it's a lot of things . . . the person I became in Brockport and also all the Sam memories. Did I tell you I ran into Rachel?"

"Bitch," Mara says, rolling her eyes.

"It's not Rachel's fault. *I'm* the one who pushed Sam away and kissed Amos and fucked everything up."

"She didn't have to say you *wrecked* him."

"Well, I deserved that."

Mara hands me a piece of streusel. "So why is Aimee suddenly the big destination?"

"What do you mean?" I peel up a wilted slice of apple and pop it into my mouth. "I haven't seen her in a year and a half, and she didn't come to graduation—"

"Exactly," Mara says. "She didn't come to graduation because she has this pattern of letting you down. No offense, but why drive all the way out there when she might hurt you again. Is that what you need right now?"

126

I take a sip of coffee and say, "She can't let me down this time because *I'm* the one going *there*, so it's not like I'll be waiting around for her to show up."

"I guess."

"Maybe you can't understand this because you grew up with two parents who never left your side for eighteen years, and you've lived in the same house since you were born, and, hey, you actually know your father's last name . . ." I pause for a second. I know I'm being harsh, but that's how Mara and I are with each other. She's given it to me this way before, actually a lot worse. It stings in the moment, but we both agree it's better to clear the air than leave stuff unsaid. "At the end of the day," I add, "Aimee is all I have, so I can't exactly write her off even if everyone else thinks she's a big flake."

Mara shakes her head. "That's bullshit."

"Which part?"

"That Aimee is all you have. You have me and my parents. You have lots of people."

"Who else?" I ask. "Seriously . . . let me know because I'm curious."

When Mara doesn't respond, I say, "We moved so much that I've always lost everyone. I think at some point I realized that it hurt too much to get close to people. It's easier to have, you know, quick things. Shallow things."

"So shallow you're drowning," Mara murmurs.

"What's that supposed to mean?"

Mara shrugs. "When you said that you don't let your-self get close to people . . . are you talking about Sam?"

"I don't want to talk about Sam."

"Fine," Mara says. "But you didn't *lose* all those people. You just moved. You always had the option of staying in touch."

"Like pen pals?" I laugh sarcastically. "No . . . I lost them."

Mara sips her coffee, and we stare across the park at this squirrel frantically digging a hole in the dirt. After a minute she turns to me. "Listen . . . I'm sorry. I just don't want to see you get hurt again."

"Maybe I will," I say. "Maybe Aimee will bail on me and I'll have to deal . . . but in the end, it's not like I'm that much different from her. I'm running away just like she does. And look how I let people down. Look how I let Sam down."

"You let Sam down because you were scared."

"Of what?"

"Of allowing him to love you . . . of admitting that you love him back."

When Mara says that, my stomach flips over. I set my coffee on the bench and touch my hands to my cheeks.

Mara glances over at me. "We don't have to talk about Sam if you don't want to."

I take a deep breath and exhale slowly.

"By the way," she adds, "I don't think you're like Aimee."

"Thanks," I say quietly.

Mara reaches over and pats my shoulder, and then we just sit there for a while, watching the squirrel pry a nut out of the ground and carry it into a tree.

14

"Okay," I say, reaching across the table for the canister of crushed red pepper. "I'm ready to talk about Sam."

Mara sets down her forkful of pizza. "Seriously?"

I nod quickly and glance around the restaurant. It's seven thirty in the evening, and Mara and I are eating at Pizza Hut. Not that I was having pangs for my former workplace. Basically, Mara and I were total tourists today. We went to Millennium Park, where we checked out this giant metal sculpture that's so shiny you can see your reflection staring back at you. When we left there, we meandered down Michigan Avenue, browsing in and out of shops. Mara got a funky beaded headband and we bought matching lime-green tank tops. We paid a gazillion dollars to ride this insanely fast elevator to the top of the Hancock building, but it was totally worth it because the sky was so clear and open we could see all the way to

Wisconsin. When we hit the bottom, we splurged on tall cups of Jamba Juice, which we sipped as we sat in the plaza, people-watching and soaking in the sunshine.

By dinnertime we both realized we'd blown way too much cash. Mara suggested going back to her place and having chips and salsa for dinner. That's when I remembered my Pizza Hut gift card. We took the train a few stops and, well, here we are.

"So," Mara says. "Sam."

I drink some iced tea and explain my theory about how, for one, I pushed him away because so far in my life my main experience with love, meaning my mom, has taught me that it hurts. And, for two, I could never let Sam get to know the real me because, deep down, I suck and I didn't want him to figure that out.

When I'm done, Mara traces her finger around the rim of her cup.

"What?" I push my hair behind my ears. "Do you agree? Or am I full of shit?"

"You want the truth?"

"Of course."

Mara wipes her lips with her napkin. "I'd say semi-full of shit. For one, you don't suck. Look at everything you've done. Getting into Bost—"

"Off the wait list," I say.

"Getting into BU and kicking ass in those school plays. You have to know how talented you are. And driving all the way to Tex—"

131

"I haven't made it to Texas yet."

"You've made it to Chicago, and I seriously wouldn't have the guts to drive six hundred miles by myself." Mara breaks off a piece of pizza with the edge of her fork. "And for two, I think Sam *did* know the real you."

"What do you mean?"

"Remember when I came home last month and we all went to the Lilac Festival?"

"Yeah?"

"And remember how I said I'd never seen you that happy?"

"Yeah?"

"What I meant was that I'd never seen you that calm, especially around a guy. But when you were with Sam, it seemed like you weren't putting on any act. You were just *you*, and Sam loved you for it."

I poke at an ice cube with my straw. The server comes over with drink refills. As soon as she's gone, Mara squeezes some lemon into her cup. I dump in a packet of sugar and say, "I still don't know if I could have been this perfect girlfriend for him. I don't think life is a fairy tale that way. You don't get hit on the head with a hockey puck and fall into the lap of Prince Charming and he saves you and everything is changed forever."

"Maybe it doesn't happen in a fairy-tale second," Mara says. "But maybe you meet someone and you really like him and gradually certain things start to change in your life and, one day, you realize you're able to let him in."

"Maybe," I say, slurping some iced tea, "but I'm not convinced."

"He's totally, completely gay," I declare.

"No way!" Mara shrieks.

"Gay."

"Take it back."

"Gay."

"Will you please stop saying that?"

Mara and I are in her room, reading the online profile of the guy from her yoga class. We were about to go to sleep, but then Mara popped out of bed, turned on her laptop, and said that since I'm leaving tomorrow morning, she needed some tips for landing Camel Guy. But as soon as I saw his picture and read his information, my gaydar went into high alert.

"How do you know?" Mara asks. "It doesn't *say* he's gay."

"Maybe he doesn't know yet. Or maybe he doesn't want his parents to know. But believe me, this guy is totally—"

"Don't!"

I turn to Mara. "What about Navneet?"

"From Starbucks?"

"He definitely seemed like he was into you."

Mara gazes dreamily at her gay fantasy boyfriend.

"Navneet is cute," I add.

"Maybe," she says, "but he's so skinny. . . ."

"Skinny is good."

Mara raises her eyebrows at me.

"You can *feed* skinny," I say, "but you can't change someone's sexual orientation."

"Now I'm depressed." Mara stands up and heads toward the door. "I'm going to take a shower."

"Think about Navneet in there!" I shout.

I can hear the bathroom door close and the water start up. I type my password into Mara's laptop and send a quick e-mail to Aimee's friends in Springfield. I let them know I'm planning to sleep over in St. Louis tomorrow and will arrive at their house around noon on Saturday. Then I e-mail my mom and tell her I should be in San Antonio by early next week. I'm about to log off, but then I decide to scroll through my contact list and . . . there it is.

Michael's e-mail address.

Back when we lived in San Diego, we'd sometimes IM each other, making dinner plans or arranging when he'd pick me up from a friend's house. Before I can stop myself, I click on his address and start writing.

To: michael_blaustein
From: VVV927
Date: Thursday, July 14 10:51 P.M.
Subject: hello from chicago

Michael—

Hey, it's V. Remember me? I was thinking about you recently and just wanted to see how it's going. How's

Mama? Do you still take her to that beach? I miss doing that.

Well, I don't know what else to say. I was living with my grandparents since I left San Diego, but now I'm driving to Texas to see my mom. But you probably don't want to hear about that, so I won't get into it or anything.

I hope your life is going well. Oh, I'm going to Boston University in the fall. I'm hoping to do a lot of theater stuff. Maybe someday I'll be on one of your TV shows???

Anyway, I hope it isn't too weird that I'm writing to you.

Take care,
V

As soon as I'm done, I hit SEND and stare at the screen for a while. I thought I'd feel all panicky and wish I could reach into cyberspace and yank the e-mail back. But the strange thing is that now that I've written to Michael, I'm wondering why on earth I waited so long.

15

It's three hundred miles from Chicago to St. Louis, and I'm determined not to get lost. Before I leave Mara's, I study my atlas and mark the route down I-55 with a yellow highlighter. I even write the directions on a Post-it to stick onto my dashboard in case the traffic is too crazy for me to be able to look at the map.

Mara fills a bottle of water for me, chills two cans of Coke, and lets me take the Pizza Hut leftovers. As she's packing my snacks, I go online and make a reservation at a hotel on the outskirts of St. Louis. It's cheap, right off the highway, and none of the customer reviews say anything about mice or midnight howling.

Once I'm in my car, I plug my iPod into the stereo, sip the first Coke, and sing along with the music when I know the words. As I leave Chicago, it's all factories and sprawling industrial warehouses. But after an hour or so, I'm surrounded by nothing but cornfields, soybean fields, and the wide blue sky. And it's so flat I can actually see entire trains off in the distance, chugging their cargo through the countryside. Also, I keep spotting these weathered old farmhouses and I imagine how they've probably looked exactly the same for the past century, generations of children waking up in those same bedrooms, pressing their faces against those same windows, and staring out at those same fields.

I used to get that feeling in Brockport, when I was wandering along the Erie Canal or crossing the lift bridge or passing that stone house that has a post out front where people used to tie horses. Sam pointed it out to me as we were walking to Luca's one evening. The funny thing is I'd driven down that street a million times and had never noticed the post before.

I'm reading a billboard for the Abraham Lincoln Presidential Library when my phone rings. It's in the middle of the passenger seat, so I reach for it, but then change my mind and leave it sitting there untouched. I'm in a good groove right now, and I don't feel like having anything change that.

I drink the second Coke from Mara. I adjust the rearview mirror. I'm polishing off the cold pizza when Sam's song comes on. I consider skipping over it, but I brace myself and listen anyway.

I've definitely been thinking a lot about Sam today. Partially, it's the stuff Mara and I were talking about. But also, every time I see a sign counting down the mileage to

St. Louis, it reminds me of this joke we used to have. It started at the cast party for *Chicago,* when the director had us reach into a hat filled with DVDs of old-time musicals. I pulled out this one from the 1940s called *Meet Me in St. Louis.* The next night Sam and I curled up on my couch and watched the movie together. Actually, we didn't catch the second half because as soon as my grandparents went to bed, we started kissing and the next thing we knew the credits were rolling. From then on whenever Sam and I made a plan to meet at my locker or his house or wherever, we'd say, *Or maybe we should meet in St. Louis?* If anyone else was listening, they'd give us a strange look, but we'd just crack up.

As I'm crossing the Mississippi River, I spot that enormous silvery arch that marks my arrival in St. Louis. According to *Let's Go USA,* this is the famous Gateway to the West. I grab my phone and snap a photo.

I'm a few miles from my hotel when I notice a Whole Foods off the next exit. I hit my blinker and cross two lanes. Aimee had a boyfriend in Oregon who was obsessed with Whole Foods. He called it Whole Paycheck because everything costs so much, but it's so delicious. His name was Elias and he was a wanker, but even I had to admit their food rocked. It's healthy and organic, but not in the bulgur and barley kind of way.

I find a parking spot and slip my feet into my flip-flops. As soon as I'm inside, I grab a basket and head to prepared foods, where I load up on seared veggie dumplings, Thai chicken satay, shrimp quesadillas, and a container of pasta salad. After that I hit produce and toss in a box of raspberries and a bag of fresh cherries.

I know this is going to be insanely expensive, but I've already decided to use the money Linda gave me on my last night at Pizza Hut. She said it was to treat myself to something special. I can't believe I'm admitting this, but after a thousand miles of Pringles and pretzels and Pop-Tarts, I'm actually craving something real. Also, I'm going to dig out that cooler from my grandparents and fill it with ice at the hotel. That way I can stretch these groceries through dinner tonight and a few meals tomorrow.

I'm on my way to the registers when I smell the bakery. I wander past the multigrain rolls and picholine olive focaccias, remembering all the breads Sam used to bake. Sourdough was his favorite. Before I can stop myself, I grab a sourdough baguette and head to the checkout line.

The dumplings rock. The chicken rocks. The quesadillas rock. The pasta salad rocks. The sourdough baguette rocks.

I'm sitting at the small table in my hotel room, sampling bites of everything. The outside of this place is shabby, but the room is actually okay. If you have a thing for cupids, of course. It's a regular room with a bed and a dresser and a TV cabinet, but there are naked, arrow-wielding boys adorning the wallpaper, a stuffed cupid doll reclining on the pillow, and five or six cupid candles on the bedside table.

It definitely seems strange that a hotel would encourage candle usage, but as I was checking in, the woman at the desk handed me a key on an angel-winged chain and a pack of matches.

"Matches?" I asked.

"Light a candle," she said breathily. "Light many candles."

I stared at her, wondering whether this was an insurance scam, enticing guests to burn down the building so she could collect the cash. But she just smiled, gestured toward my room, and said, "This is your night, dear."

After I'm done eating, I pile all the containers into the cooler, on top of a mound of ice. Then I flop onto the bed, shove the cupid doll off to one side, and reach for my phone. I should probably try my grandparents. They were the ones who called while I was driving today. Then again, I'm still not in the mood to deal with them. I click on the photo of the Gateway Arch and write them a text message about how I'm in St. Louis and will call tomorrow.

I text Linda and thank her again for the money and let her know the trip is going well so far. I hesitate for a second, wondering whether she's found out that I hooked up with Nate. He didn't seem like the kiss-and-tell type. At least I hope not.

I'm about to close my phone, but then I open the

photo of the arch again and enter Sam's number. I consider writing: *Meet me in St. Louis.* But then I think about how by tomorrow I'll be in rural Missouri and the next day I'll be in Oklahoma and the next day I'll be cruising through Texas, so I quickly type: *Meet me in the middle of nowhere.* That seems more appropriate given this drive and the basic state of how Sam and I left things.

I stare at the message for a long time, thinking, *Should I or shouldn't I?* What if he writes me back? What would I say? Or what if he doesn't? Either way, I'm not ready to handle it.

I delete the message to Sam, plug my phone into the charger, and head into the shower. I shampoo my hair and massage in extra conditioner. I shave my legs. I dry off with a towel and put on my new tank top from Chicago. I brush my teeth, tweeze some stray hairs from my eyebrows, and rub moisturizer onto my shins. I pull back the comforter on the bed and reach for the remote. But then I set it down again and grab the matches instead. I light two candles, slide between the starched sheets, and stare up at the shadows flickering on the ceiling.

I slip my hand past my stomach and start rubbing between my legs. As I'm touching myself, I think about how I'm doing this for *me.* Not to impress some guy or turn him on with my footloose and free-loving ways. And that, more than anything, feels really, really good.

16

I haven't seen the Tanners since I was eight, but the instant I step onto their front lawn, they feel like family. Melissa and Drew were Aimee's friends in Seattle. We all lived in the same building. Melissa was in med school and Drew was getting his Ph.D., so they were as broke as we were. On warm evenings we'd sit on the roof and eat Oreos and complain about their professors and my third-grade teacher and Aimee's boss.

Ever since we left Seattle, Aimee and Melissa exchanged occasional e-mails and vowed to visit, but so far it has never happened. At some point we learned that Melissa became a neurologist, Drew got a job at a college in the Midwest, and they had a daughter named Bella Rose.

It took me four hours to get from St. Louis to their tiny town outside of Springfield, Missouri. They meet me in the driveway and take turns hugging me and commenting on how beautiful I look, so tall, such long hair. I hug them back and, I have to admit, I'm soaking up the praise.

Drew grabs my suitcase and Melissa takes my hand and we head into the house. Melissa and Drew load the kitchen table with breads, salads, deviled eggs, and leftover barbecue chicken. As we're talking, Bella hovers near the sliding-glass door, stroking a sandy mutt and eyeing me curiously.

"Please make yourself at home," Melissa says.

"We mean that," Drew says, pointing out where I can find plates, forks, and glasses.

I pour myself some iced tea and stir in a spoonful of sugar. It's funny to see Melissa and Drew looking like grown-ups. They're probably the same age as Aimee, so when we lived in Seattle, they must have been in their mid-twenties. Melissa had long brown hair and Drew had wild curls. Now her hair is layered and his is sheared close and graying around the temples.

Bella, who is almost six, has a tangled ponytail, a freckled nose, and cut-off shorts. As we're eating lunch, she's still shy, but by the time I return from my car with the bag of cherries, I've learned that she loves the Judy Moody books, hates her middle name, and loves horses.

As I'm dumping the cherries into a bowl, Melissa says, "So how long are you staying?"

I shrug. "Probably just overnight. After this, I'm driving to Oklahoma City."

"I don't know if this would work, then." Melissa glances at Drew. "But we may as well run it by you."

I listen as Melissa explains how their regular sitter just flew to Mexico because her sister had a baby. Drew is in charge of a writing program at the college, so he can't take the week off. Melissa was going to bring Bella to her office, but then I e-mailed and said I was coming and, well, they hatched a new idea.

"Feel free to say no," Drew says, "but would you like to hang out with Bella this week? Christina promised she'll be back by next Monday."

"We'd pay you, of course," Melissa adds.

"You wouldn't have to pay me."

"We'd insist," Melissa says. "We don't have a guest room, but you can sleep on the sofa bed. And Drew has a flexible schedule in the afternoons, so you guys can go swimming at the lake. Or you can even do your own thing then."

I glance around the kitchen. The fridge is wallpapered with Bella's crayon renderings of horses. On the way in, I noticed the living room was filled with photos and shelves of books. Through the rear window, I can see pastures and hills and that endless blue sky.

"I should call Aimee first," I say, "in case she has anything planned."

"Of course," Melissa says.

"You don't have to rush the decision," Drew adds.

I eat a cherry, set the pit on my plate, and take a sip of iced tea.

"I'm so glad we get to see you," Melissa says, "however long you can stay."

I help clear the table, but they insist on doing the dishes. As Melissa washes and Drew dries, I dig my phone out of my bag.

"Why don't you use our room?" Drew says.

Melissa gestures down the hall. "Feel free to close the door, make yourself comfortable."

I head into their bedroom, kick off my flip-flops, and sit cross-legged on the faded patchwork quilt. I scroll through for Aimee's number and then hit TALK.

One ring, two rings, three rings, four rings, five rings . . .
Damn.

I hate that I always have to wonder with Aimee.

"V!" she shouts after the sixth ring. "I had my phone on vibrate and then I couldn't find it. So where are you?"

"I'm at the Tanners'. Can you believe it?"

"Oh, my God," Aimee says. "How are they? Has it really been ten years? How do they look?"

I describe their house and Bella and their backyard and how Melissa and Drew pretty much seem like real adults.

"Huh," Aimee murmurs.

After a moment I say, "I have a quick question."

"Sure . . . what's up?"

I explain how Melissa and Drew asked if I could babysit Bella this week, which means I wouldn't arrive in San Antonio until next Monday or so.

"I really want to see you," I add, "but it might be nice to get some time here. They live way out in the country. It seems really peaceful."

"Of course that's fine. I know how much you used to love them in Seattle."

"So you're not mad?"

"We've waited this long," Aimee says. "We can wait another week."

I know it's the answer I wanted, but when Aimee says that, I get this flash of anger and I want to say, *YOU weren't the one waiting. You were the one not showing up.*

"There's something I need to run by you, too," Aimee says.

"Yeah?" I ask hesitantly.

"Remember how Steve had that kidney stone last month?"

It's obviously a rhetorical question, but I'm tempted to say, *How could I forget? It's the reason you missed graduation.* But it's been so long and Aimee and I are almost together again, so I don't want to screw anything up at this point.

"Well, ever since then . . ." Aimee pauses. "Ever since then, I guess you could say things have been a little tense."

When I don't say anything, Aimee continues. "It's like it was this big life-changing experience for him, and he suddenly wants to talk about the future and . . . you know me." Aimee laughs. "I'm a live-for-the-moment kind of—"

"I can still come stay with you, right?"

"Of course! I just wanted to give you a heads-up."

"Oh," I say.

As Aimee describes how we're going to visit the River Walk and the Alamo and maybe even SeaWorld, I pick at my toenail polish. Finally, she tells me to keep her posted about my driving schedule, and then we say good-bye.

After we hang up, I stare at the framed wedding picture of Melissa and Drew on the bedside table. They're on some beach and they're all decked out except for their bare feet. They have their arms wrapped around each other and they're kissing and the sun is setting and everything looks so romantic and the best thing is that you know it's not bullshit and they didn't get divorced seven minutes after the photo was developed.

17

Every morning after Melissa and Drew leave for work, Bella and I walk down this long, dusty road to visit a horse named Crispo. We bring quartered apples and slices of carrots. As Bella braids his mane, I lean against the fence, close my eyes, and aim my face toward the sun.

By noon it's hot and muggy, so Bella and I pour glasses of lemonade and dodge into the shade on the back porch. I read *Judy Moody Predicts the Future* to Bella and we play hangman and she teaches me the latest "Miss Susie" clapping choreography.

Most afternoons Drew and Bella go to this nearby lake. One day I join them and Drew gets us ice-cream cones and we rent a canoe and paddle far out into the water. But usually I take a shower and then read or doze off on the back porch for a few hours.

In the evenings Drew barbecues on the grill while Melissa returns calls to her patients. Bella brushes the dog and attempts to tie ribbons around his ears. On Monday I help Drew shuck corn and poke veggies onto shish-kebab sticks. On Tuesday I devour a compilation of mystery stories I found on their shelf. On Wednesday I'm lounging on the steps, painting my toenails a sherbet shade of orange, when Bella comes barreling around the side yard, shouting, "V! V! There's someone here to see you!"

For some crazy reason, I think it's Sam and my heart starts pounding, even though that's completely irrational because I never sent him that text message, and even if I did, it's not like he could locate me in the middle of nowhere. Though I guess if he called my grandparents and they gave him Aimee's number and Aimee passed on the Tanners' address and—

"It's the mailman," Bella says, "but he's wearing a different color outfit."

I rise from my chair and follow Bella to the driveway.

It turns out to be a FedEx from Aimee. She's sent me this box with two packages of Oreos and a note that says:

Hey, everyone—
I wish I were there, too! Enjoy the cookies and we'll
all see each other soon enough.
Love,
Aim

That night, after Bella has gone to bed, we grab the Oreos and return to the back porch. Drew pours us glasses of milk, and as Melissa pries a cookie in half and scrapes out the filling with her teeth, I comment on how I eat my Oreos that same way.

"I know," Melissa says. "I was the one who insisted it was the best method, up on that roof in Seattle."

"Really?"

"Yeah." Melissa giggles. "I guess I created a bad habit, huh?"

We end up staying on the porch for hours. The sky is swirling with stars. Frogs are croaking and crickets are chirping, and I can't help feeling drawn into Melissa and Drew's world, with all their security and closeness. And the strange thing is that I don't feel suffocated, like I usually do around families. I guess I could say I'm even liking it.

Melissa talks about being a doctor. Drew tells me about his students. I describe Brockport and, before that, San Diego and, before that, Oregon and Louisiana and Vermont. After a while we start reminiscing about Seattle. Melissa says that I was such a cute kid, really funny and independent. Drew mentions how he was so surprised that first time he saw me in the laundry room of our building, my tiptoes on a crate, stuffing towels into the washer.

"I'm sure it was an adventure growing up with Aimee," Drew says.

Melissa shoots him a look. "You know we love your mom."

"Of course we love her," Drew says. "We were both so

stressed in Seattle, with Melissa's school and my dissertation. Aimee was our break from reality. Remember how she'd do anything in five minutes' notice?"

"Like that time we packed her car and went camping at those hot springs on the Olympic Peninsula," Melissa says.

"Or that time we drove to Oregon in the middle of the night because some band was playing at Mount Hood and Aimee was convinced we could get tickets. Do you remember that? You were sleeping in the backseat the whole time."

"It definitely sounds like Aimee," I say.

"She was so spontaneous," Melissa says.

"Is she still like that?" Drew asks.

"I guess." I shrug. "I haven't seen her for a while."

"Not since you moved in with your grandparents?" Melissa asks.

I nod.

"That must have been rough," Drew says.

"Yeah," I say. "It was."

We're all quiet for a minute. A cow is mooing off in some pasture, and every time it does, a dog start barking like crazy.

"It sounds like it turned out to be a positive thing," Melissa says. "I mean, you're heading to college next month."

I take a deep breath and stare up at the stars, and suddenly something dawns on me. I always assumed Aimee shipped me to Brockport because she wanted to get rid of me and be all footloose with that surfer guy. But maybe she sent me away for my own sake. Even I'll admit things were getting crazy in San Diego, how I was smoking all that weed and wandering around with those guys in City Heights at two in the morning. Maybe she sent me to my grandparents because she thought they could get me under control. Maybe she sent me to my grandparents because she didn't want me to turn out like her.

On Friday night I can't fall asleep. I'm leaving in the morning and I guess I'm ready, but it's also been such a nice week, such an escape. Also, I can't stop thinking about Aimee. On some level I've been angry at her for moving us so much and not showing up all those times. But after my epiphany the other night, I'm beginning to forgive her. Also, now that I've had this time with Bella, I'm realizing how much work it is to take care of a kid. Aimee was so young when she had me, practically my age. If I had to give her the benefit of the doubt, I'd say she did an okay job.

I switch on the light and thumb through the cartoons in an old issue of the *New Yorker*, but my brain won't stop racing. Finally, I crawl out of bed and tiptoe into the kitchen. Drew keeps his laptop on the table, and he's been letting me use it whenever I want. I've been IM-ing with Mara, who has informed me that she and that guy from Starbucks are planning to hang out on Sunday night.

I turn on Drew's computer and pour myself a glass of water. Mara isn't online right now, so I quickly check my e-mail. *Oh, my God!* I can't believe it. Michael wrote me back.

To: VVV927
From: michael_blaustein
Date: Friday, July 22 9:13 P.M.
Subject: of course i remember you

V—

I just returned from a hiking trip in the Sierras, but I wanted to write and say how wonderful it was to get your e-mail. One of the most painful parts about my breakup with your mom was losing you. I'm not sure how much to get into here, but I assumed you needed your space, so I purposefully stayed away.

Congratulations on BU! Did you know I went to Tufts? Boston is a great student town. You're going to love it.

The biggest news here is that I'm engaged. Her name is Catherine and—get this—she's Mama's vet! I knew that dog would do me good someday. I've told her about you, and she says she hopes to meet you someday. Hey, if you ever need a place to stay in

San Diego, our home is your home. I really mean
that.

Anyway, I've got to do laundry and (finally) make a
real cup of coffee, so I should jump off. But I hope this
is the first of many e-mails. Please stay in touch, V.
I mean that, too.

Love,
Michael

As soon as I'm done reading Michael's e-mail, I take a
sip of water and hit REPLY.

To: michael_blaustein
From: VVV927
Date: Friday, July 22 11:27 P.M.
Subject: congrats!

Hey, Michael—

Congrats on getting engaged!!! I'll write more soon,
but I just wanted to say that you didn't lose me.

Love,
V

*   *   *

On Saturday morning Melissa, Drew, Bella, and I all gather on the front lawn. They're taking a picnic to the lake for the day, and they've invited me along. Part of me wants to join them, but I'm ready to push on toward Texas and see my mom.

"Thanks for letting me stay here," I say. "And for, well, everything."

Last night Drew made this farewell meal with barbecue ribs and grilled artichokes and strawberry shortcake for dessert. And then this morning, Melissa handed me a card saying how much they loved getting to know me again and how great I was with Bella. Inside, she'd enclosed more cash than I felt comfortable accepting. When I tried returning it, Melissa said, "Consider it a graduation present, ten years of birthdays, and babysitting money all rolled into one."

"You didn't have to pay me for watching Bella."

"I know," Melissa said, touching my arm.

As I open my car door, Bella gives me a drawing of a horse and two girls, one tall and one short.

"It's you, me, and Crispo," she says.

"I recognized us right away."

We all hug and then I tuck Bella's picture into the glove compartment and pull onto the main road.

18

I'm already planning my escape.

I've just arrived in Oklahoma City. It was a long trek from Missouri, full of traffic, trucks, and tollbooths. But I was so chilled from my week at the Tanners' that it didn't get to me. I even had this totally un-me peaceful moment where I pulled over at a rest stop to work a knot out of my thigh. I was pacing up and down the sidewalk, and it was so hot and dusty and the sun was a huge ball of fire in the western sky and no one else was around and the only sounds were the whizzing of speeding cars and the faint screeching of a nearby oil well, and the crazy thing is that I was actually okay with it. Being alone and the silence and everything. I stayed there for several minutes, stretching my muscles, listening to everything and nothing.

But now, as I wander the lobby of this budget hotel I found in *Let's Go USA*, I'm getting more and more agitated. I can't seem to locate the elevator and, to make matters worse, I keep ending up at this hideous indoor fountain. Yes, a *fountain*. It's got a statue of a boy balancing a sparrow on his outstretched arm. The water is trickling out of the boy's ears and dripping into a mucky birdbath.

In keeping with the avian theme, the woman who checked me in said I'm the only guest who isn't participating in the Bird Photographers of Oklahoma convention this weekend. As if she had to tell me. I'm circling the lobby, and I keep stumbling into middle-aged people toting camera equipment and wearing T-shirts that proclaim YOU TRY FLYING THOUSANDS OF MILES EVERY YEAR.

Finally, I sidestep three otherwise-normal-looking men making shrill birdcalls, take a sharp left, and find myself facing an open elevator. I rush in and hurriedly push 6. Once I'm in the room, I thought I would be relieved, but I actually don't feel any better. For one, it's icy cold and I can't turn down the air conditioner and the windows won't crack an inch. I could go for a stroll, but it's a million degrees out and, besides, the hotel is flanked by highways. The woman at the desk said there was a mall nearby. Then again, I shouldn't blow any money. I have that cash from the Tanners, but I need to save it for the drive home and my first semester at college. Unless, of course, I can earn money while I'm in San Antonio. My mom told me the other night that she'll try to get me a short-term gig bussing tables at the restaurant where she works. Then again, she wasn't definite about it, so I should hang on to my money for now.

All in all, the hardest part about being trapped in this hotel room is knowing that I'm only 466 miles from San Antonio. That'd take me about eight or nine hours. I glance at the clock: 4:46 P.M. If I left now, I could be with my mom by one or two in the morning.

I've already been driving all day, so it'd make more sense to leave tomorrow. Actually, I told my mom I wouldn't be there until Monday because I assumed I'd sleep over in Dallas. But if I do some hardcore driving, I could totally make it in one day. *Oh, my God.* Tomorrow at this time, my mom and I will be hanging out in her house. Maybe she'll make that pasta salad for me. She can tell me about Costa Rica and Florida and the Georgia coast, and I can tell her about Brockport and Sam. Maybe she'll have remembered some vital facts about my father. When I think about that, my stomach gets all fluttery and nervous.

I dig out my phone and dial Aimee to let her know my revised plans. Just voice mail. I leave a message, telling her to call me immediately, and then I stretch out on the bed and attempt to read a book of short stories from Melissa. I totally can't concentrate, so I dig through my suitcase for my bathing suit. *Let's Go* said there's a pool on the deck off the fourth floor. I throw on a T-shirt over my bikini, grab a towel, and head into the hallway. Of course, I can't find the elevator, so I walk down two flights of concrete stairs and follow signs out to the deck.

The water is glassy and still. There isn't anyone around, just a bunch of empty lounge chairs and this enormous golden statue of a sparrow. I toss my towel onto a table, dive in, and paddle to the shallow end. Then I close my eyes and float toward the deep end, push off from the wall, and swim underwater to the other side. I'm just emerging near the stucco stairs when a flock of people spill onto the deck and plunk themselves down two feet from me.

"Hey there!" an older woman shouts. "Are you native or migratory?"

I wipe the water off my face. "What?"

These two blond women, probably in their thirties, glance at each other. But then the older woman explains how they've been divided into groups to alternate their bird-watching expeditions.

"So you're not with the convention?" a man asks. I recognize him as a bird-caller from the lobby.

I shake my head.

"You can be an honorary migratory," he concludes, "like us."

I consider telling him I'd rather be native, but instead I gesture to the statue on the other side of the pool and say, "So what's up with all these sparrows?"

The two blond women stare at me like I've just asked them whether ice cream is cold.

"It's not a sparrow," the older woman says. "It's a scissor-tailed flycatcher."

"The state bird of Oklahoma," the man adds.

The older woman launches into this story about how she and her daughters, who I assume are the two blond women, have been photographing the flycatcher for the past twenty years and how it's famous for its sky dance and long scissorlike tail. I sit on the stairs, chipping the polish off my toes. For some reason, this random ornithology lesson is making me feel all emotional. I think it's watching the mom and her daughters, doing the same thing they've been doing together for the past two decades, and thinking how, even though Aimee and I never had that us-against-the-world bond, we did share a lot of memories, all those places, all those moves.

I say good-bye to the bird crew, step out of the pool, and grab my towel. I sprint up the two flights of stairs and into my room, where I peel off my bikini and pull on a sundress. Then I stuff everything into my suitcase and run back down the stairs.

"Checking out so soon?" asks the woman at the front desk.

I twist my wet hair into a ponytail and say, "Yeah . . . change of plans."

"I can talk to my manager about a refund, but I don't think—"

"Don't worry about it."

I hand her my room card, head to my car, and pull back onto the highway. I take Kilpatrick Turnpike until I get to 35 South. In order to get to San Antonio, I'm going

160

to have to drive nearly five hundred miles through the night. But I've waited a year and a half to see my mom, and right now I don't want to wait any longer.

I drive for two straight hours. I pass car dealerships and strip malls. I pass Wal-Marts and Dollar Tree stores. I pass signs for casinos and signs for Gamblers Anonymous. After a while the landscape gets more remote, just sky, plains, and the occasional dust cloud.

The horizon is streaked with reds and oranges. It's the most incredible sunset I've ever seen. I try my mom's phone a few more times, but it keeps bouncing right to voice mail. I leave her a message that I'll be arriving in San Antonio later tonight, so I need directions to her house.

As the sky turns darker and my car climbs into the rocky hills of southern Oklahoma, I lose cell-phone reception. *Damn.* I still haven't heard back from my mom. Then again, I have three hundred miles left to go, so I'm sure she'll call at some point.

It's eight thirty as I cross the border into Texas. I'm hungry and thirsty and low on gas, and even though my phone is working again, I still haven't heard anything and it's starting to stress me out. I really do need my mom's address, especially since I don't know Steve's last name, so I can't even call directory assistance.

I exit the highway and head toward a truck stop. Everywhere I look, there are neon signs for triple-X movies and fantasy hot spots. If my grandparents knew where I was, they'd croak. We didn't discuss their stance on porn-filled strips, but I did promise them I wouldn't drive at night.

As soon as I step out of the car, some guys by the gas pumps hoot at me in Spanish. I want to tell them to fuck off, but the only phrase I remember from Spanish class is *Where's the train station?* so I lock the door and head inside.

As I'm waiting in line at Subway, I notice that the man in front of me is wearing a ten-gallon hat. The three women behind me, in skintight jeans and cowboy boots, are comparing notes about firearms. I am definitely not in Brockport anymore.

I eat a roast beef sub and carry a jumbo Coke back to the car. The hecklers are gone, so I drive over to the pumps, fill up my tank, and leave another message for Aimee. Then I open my atlas and trace my finger down to Dallas, through Austin, all the way to San Antonio.

Somewhere south of Waco, I'm so tired I want to die.

It's past midnight. Even though the traffic was congested around Fort Worth, there's hardly anyone on the road now, just a few lonely rigs chugging through the night.

I can't believe how far I've driven today. It's been three hundred miles since Oklahoma City. And then, with my earlier trip from Missouri, I've done more than six hundred miles in less than twenty-four hours.

I'm blasting my music and sipping the warm, watery Coke and slapping my cheeks to stay awake when, all of a sudden, my phone rings. I swerve to the right, turn down the volume, and glance at the caller ID: AIMEE.

"Hang on a sec!" I shout into the phone. There's an exit coming up, so I quickly turn off, steer down the frontage road, and pull into an empty rest stop. This way, I can find paper and write down the directions to my mom's house.

As soon as I've parked, I pick up the phone again. "Where have you been? Didn't you get my messages?"

"I haven't had a chance to check. . . ." my mom says. Her voice is groggy, like she's been sleeping for a long time. "I noticed some missed calls and—"

"Guess what? I've just driven through Waco, so I'm about three hours from San Antonio. Can you believe it? I was at my hotel, and I realized I was so close, I should just go for it."

"Oh no."

"Why?" I ask. "What's wrong?"

"I'm actually . . . I'm on Padre Island. I didn't think you were coming until Monday."

I tighten my grip on the phone. "Where's that?"

"Oh, hon . . ." She blows her nose. "Steve and I broke up yesterday morning, and I needed to get away. You know how it is. . . ."

"Where's Padre Island?"

"He'll be staying with his brother for a few weeks while I figure out my plans, but I was knocking around that house and—"

"Where's Padre Island?" I ask again.

"It's two hundred and fifty miles south of San Antonio . . . right near the Mexican border."

"I still have a few more hours," I say, "so if you leave now, we could both arrive in San Antonio around the same time."

Aimee doesn't respond. In the long silence that follows, I have this feeling that now, more than ever, is our moment of truth. I'm basically saying, *I've traveled nearly two thousand miles for you. So do you love me enough to drive a few hours for me?*

Aimee blows her nose again. "Oh, hon," she says, "I don't think that's going to work. I wasn't planning on having you until Monday. I've paid for this place, and I'm just not in the best shape right now."

"What am I supposed to do? It's the middle of the night, and I'm on the side of some deserted road and—" My voice catches. I swallow hard and then say, "No, forget it. I'll figure it out."

"I'm sure you will." Aimee clears her throat. "I know this is hard . . . but please try to understand. I just need a little time. On Monday we can meet up in San Antonio, and I'll take you to this nice lunch place. I can call in the morning and make a reservation. Does that sound okay?"

I say okay, but as soon as we hang up, I start crying. I'm crying so hard, my chest is heaving. I cry and cry, and, eventually, I stop crying, cut the engine, and fall asleep.

When I wake up, the sky is pink. There's a field of parched brown grass off to one side. A seat-belt buckle is ramming into my hip and my head is pounding and it's so hot my thighs are sticking together.

At first I don't know where I am. But then I taste last night's sandwich in my mouth and I smell chlorine in my hair and my throat tightens and my eyes fill with tears. Before I can stop myself, I grab my phone and do something I never thought I'd do.

"Hello?"

As soon as I hear my grandma's voice, I start crying all over again.

"V? Honey? Are you okay?"

I catch my breath long enough to gasp, "I'm . . . I . . . can you and Grandpa talk?"

"Of course we can," my grandma says. "Hold on a second."

As soon as my grandpa picks up, I explain, between sobs, how I was driving through the night to see Aimee, but she's in some place called Padre Island and doesn't want to come back until Monday and I'm on the side of the highway and I honestly don't know where to go from here. I assume they're going to lay into me for driving at night or say something like, *We knew Aimee would do this,* but as soon as I'm done talking, my grandpa says, "Would you like us to fly out there? We can be on a plane in the next few hours. We'll stay with you until Aimee returns."

"Or would you like us to call Aimee?" my grandma asks. "We could persuade her to come back today."

"I don't think so," I say quietly. "I don't want anyone to have to *persuade* her to see me."

"How about this?" my grandma says. "We'll call a hotel in San Antonio and book you a room. You can relax, get some sleep, and by Monday Aimee will be back."

"I don't know," I say. "I mean, I can do that my-my-my—" I collapse into sobs again.

"We know you can do it yourself," my grandma says. "But we *want* to do this for you. We want to help."

"Call us back in ten minutes," my grandpa says.

After we hang up, I wipe away the tears and fiddle with my seat belt and stare out at the dry grass. When I call them back, my grandpa gives me directions to the Crowne Plaza San Antonio. I scribble it onto a gas-station receipt and then pull back on the highway toward San Antonio.

19

His name is Tommy, and I can already tell we're going to hook up.

"I make the best guacamole in San Antonio," he says as he stands next to my table, ready to take my order.

"How would I know for sure?" I fan myself with the menu. "I haven't tried all the guacamole in San Antonio."

"No need to. You're here. Your search has ended."

"That's a little confident, Tommy."

"Just being honest," he says. "Hey, how do you know my name?"

I take a sip of water. "I have my ways."

Tommy is a waiter at this restaurant on a second-story porch overhanging the River Walk. I spotted him as I was walking on the other side of the river, so I climbed the stone stairs, crossed the arching bridge, and asked the hostess to seat me in his section.

"All the girls want to be in Tommy's section," she said, rolling her eyes.

"So that's really your name?" I crunch on an ice cube. "I didn't realize anyone is actually called Tommy anymore."

"My dad is Thomas. My cousin is Tom. My uncle is TJ." Tommy raises his hand to his forehead in a two-fingered salute. "Born and bred in backwoods Kentucky."

"What are you doing in San Antonio?" I ask.

"Long story," he says. "Preferably told after some shots of tequila."

"Sounds good."

I order chips and guacamole. Tommy delivers drinks to a neighboring table and then pushes the guacamole cart over to me. It's loaded with avocados and pottery containers of cilantro, chopped onions, and minced jalapeños. I watch as he expertly mashes an avocado, squeezes a few wedges of lime over the bowl, and then stirs in the remaining ingredients.

"You're really serious about this," I say.

"When it comes to guacamole"—Tommy sets a basket of tortilla chips on my table—"I don't fool around."

"When do you fool around?"

Tommy grins as he hands over the guacamole.

"Save it for the tequila?" I ask.

"Exactly."

Tommy is right about his guacamole. It's definitely on

the spicy side, though, so I keep summoning him over to refill my water glass. Okay, it's not just about the water. But I don't think he minds because every time he returns, we joke around until the neighboring tables start looking neglected.

Finally, a guy with a massive platter of ribs snaps his barbecue-sauced fingers in the air. "Waiter—" he shouts. "Are you getting paid to serve food or pick up the ladies?"

Tommy pushes the guacamole cart over to that guy's table and offers him a free sample. But later, as he's handing me my bill, we make a plan to meet when his shift is done at ten.

After I leave the restaurant, I wander around the River Walk. It's cooler down here than up on the street. It's also surprisingly tranquil, with the shimmery water and mossy stonework and lazily drifting boats.

My grandparents actually picked a great hotel. The Crowne Plaza is situated right next to the River Walk. The instant I arrived at the room, I collapsed on the bed and slept for the rest of the day. When I finally woke up, I shampooed the chlorine out of my hair, hooked on my strapless push-up bra, and wriggled into that dress I bought for graduation. Then I went out to my car, where I retrieved my strappy sandals. I hadn't touched them since I hurled them into the back after that party where I kissed Amos.

Even as I was blow-drying my hair and smudging eye shadow on my lids, I wasn't admitting why I was going all out. But then I spotted Tommy pushing his guacamole cart, and it was hard to be in denial much longer.

When I meet Tommy at ten, he's changed into a clean shirt and a pair of jeans. And I didn't notice this before, but he has a silver stud through his tongue.

"Your real name is V?" he asks as we cross the bridge.

"It's actually Vivienne," I say, "but everyone calls me V."

We pause at the bottom of the stairs.

"Where do you want to go?" Tommy asks.

"You know this place better than I do. What do people want to see when they come to San Antonio?"

"Mostly the Alamo . . . but I think it's closed now."

We take a left and wander past the boutiques and restaurants. Tommy points out the fudge shop where his friend works and the bar where his buddy slips him under-age shots.

"Actually," Tommy says, pausing. "About that tequila."

"I'm right behind you."

The bouncer informs us that Tommy's friend isn't here tonight, so we head to a nearby fountain and sit on the ledge, watching the lights illuminate the water.

"Do you still want to tell me why you left Kentucky?" I ask.

"Because of a girl," Tommy says. "And a dog."

"And a truck? Should I be playing a country song?"

Tommy runs his fingers through the water and explains how he and his high-school girlfriend adopted a puppy last summer. When she decided to move to San Antonio, he knew their relationship wasn't going anywhere, but he loved the dog, so he came along. They broke up a month later, and she and the dog moved to Nebraska. Tommy thought about returning home, but he was discovering his talent with guacamole, and avocados are much harder to come by in Kentucky.

"It'll be a year in September," Tommy says.

"So you're here for the avocados?"

"As good a reason as any." Tommy dries his hand on his jeans. "What about you? Why are you in San Antonio?"

"You really want to know? It's a long, pathetic story."

Tommy shrugs. "I don't have any other plans tonight."

I tell him about my mom and how I drove all the way from New York to visit her, but she'd rather wallow on some island. I tell him how she bailed on my graduation last month and my school plays and my seventeenth birthday, which is why I'm an idiot to have traveled two thousand miles with this expectation that things would be different.

Because I'm on a roll, I tell him about Sam and how I pushed him away and then cheated on him because I was scared to love and be loved. But what I've recently realized is that even if my mom doesn't love me enough, there are a lot of people who do, myself included. Except now Sam has moved to California and probably never wants to talk to me again.

"Now *you* sound like the country song," Tommy says, and then he starts chuckling.

"Is my pathetic life that funny?"

"Sorry," Tommy says. "I just didn't think pretty blond girls had problems. It's kind of refreshing."

"I'm not that blond."

"And you don't have that many problems."

"Yes, I do," I say. "I just drove all the way to San Antonio and my mom isn't here and who knows if she'll even come back tomorrow? She could call me in the morning and tell me she needs a few more days to pull herself together and, by the way, she's in the South Pacific."

"I guess that is a problem."

"Thanks for reminding me."

We wander around the River Walk, watching couples licking ice-cream cones and mariachi bands serenading tables of tourists. After a while my sandals start rubbing the skin off my toes, so I tell Tommy I'm going to head back to the hotel.

Tommy walks me to Pecan Street, over the bridge, and up the short flight of stairs.

"Want to come in?" I ask, gesturing toward the lobby.

"Are you sure?"

"Sure," I say, nodding.

When we get to my room, I go into the bathroom, where I brush my hair and swish with mouthwash. When I come out, Tommy is sitting in a chair, looking through the room-service menu.

I flop onto the bed. "Do you want to order something?"

"Nah. I'm just seeing who makes their guacamole."

As I lean against the headboard, I think about how we're probably going to chat for the next ten minutes. Then I'll toss my hair over my shoulders and grin at Tommy, and he'll scooch closer to the bed. Maybe he'll angle in for a kiss or maybe, if he's the polite southern boy that I think he is, I'll have to advance things myself.

Suddenly, I start to cry.

"Hey, what's wrong?" Tommy asks, setting down the menu.

I wave my hand as if to say, *No big deal,* but I can't stop. And it's not just a little sniffle. I'm unleashing a flood of tears and way more snot than Tommy was hoping to see tonight. I'm crying because I'm doing exactly what I don't want to be doing anymore, using a guy to escape whatever's going on in my life. I'm crying because it won't help to hook up with Tommy, just like it didn't help to hook up with Nate, just like it didn't help to hook up with Amos. What will really help, deep down, is not to let Aimee send me into these self-destructive downward spirals. I need to acknowledge that she may have controlled my past, but she doesn't have to dominate my present and my future, too.

"I'm sorry," I say, wiping my nose. "You don't have to stay . . . really . . . You should go."

"Don't worry," Tommy says. "I'm not leaving."

"Why? I'm a mess."

Tommy kicks off his sneakers and sits next to me on the bed. "You seem like you need a friend right now."

As he slides his arm around me, I cry even harder.

"You know what I think?" Tommy grabs a few tissues off the bedside table. "I think you should call that guy and tell him you still love him."

"But I was awful to him," I say. "I told you how I cheated on him at that party. There's no way he's going to talk to me after that."

"Tell him your head was messed up because of your mom, but you're starting to figure things out and you want to make things better with him."

"You really think I could say that?"

"It's worth a try."

Tommy clicks his tongue ring across his teeth. After a minute he says, "Why did you leave New York again?"

"To come see my mom."

"But you knew he was in California, right?"

"Yeah."

"And you must have looked at a map. You've got to know that Texas is only a few states from California."

"What's that supposed to mean?"

"You said your mom always lets you down. Did you really need her to do it one more time?"

"I guess not," I say quietly.

"Maybe you were actually driving out here to see him."

It's a lot to think about. I lie back and rest my head on a pillow. Tommy starts stroking my hair. I'm just drifting off when he whispers, "I better go. I've got to work break-fast tomorrow."

I open my eyes.

"After all," he says, clicking his tongue ring, "I'm get-ting paid to serve food, not pick up the ladies."

When Tommy stands up to leave, I say, "I want to get something from my car for you."

I grab my keys and we head down in the elevator. As soon as we get to my car, I unlock the door and dig through the backseat until I find that compass my grandma insisted I bring along.

"What's this for?" Tommy asks as I hand it to him.

"For helping me find my way."

Tommy puts it in his pocket and then walks me back to the lobby and gives me a tight hug.

"Enjoy California," he says. "I hear they have great avocados out there."

As I'm checking out of the hotel, the concierge tells me there's a good breakfast place on Commerce, a block from the Alamo. I park in a nearby lot and carry my atlas inside. I sit at a table, order a cup of coffee and an egg sandwich, and stare down at the map of the United States.

There are several major highways leading out of San Antonio. There's I-35, which is how I got down here in the first place. I could always hop back on it, heading north. I could drive up through Oklahoma, Missouri, and Illinois, back along the Great Lakes, all the way to Brockport.

There's a highway to Houston and a highway to Corpus Christi and a highway to Mexico. I have a month until college starts, so I suppose I could spend the next few weeks wandering the Southwest, having random adventures.

Then I glance at 10 West. That would take me across Texas, New Mexico, and Arizona, all the way to California.

My hands are trembling as I lay some bills on the table and ask the waiter to wrap up my breakfast instead. Once he gives me the bag, I grab some napkins, close the atlas, and head out to my car.

Sam

I arrived in Berkeley on a warm Thursday in late July.

My atlas didn't have an expanded map of the East Bay, so I kept pulling over and asking people where I was. Finally, a woman with braided white hair sketched me the directions on the back of a protest flyer.

It was early evening when I parked in front of a run-down Victorian house on Shattuck Avenue. Rachel is the one who gave me Sam's address. I talked to her when I was staying with Michael and his fiancée, Catherine, in San Diego. When I told Rachel where I was headed, she whistled dramatically under her breath. But I explained how important this was, and she agreed to keep it between us. My grandparents and Mara were the only other people who knew where I was going. I called my grandpa as I was leaving San Antonio and asked him to pass a message along to Aimee that I wouldn't be making that lunch after all.

I climbed the steps and knocked on the peeling front door. No one answered. I turned and looked at my car, dusty from the desert, streaked from that sudden downpour in the mountains north of Los Angeles.

I knocked again, and in the silence that followed I wondered if I'd made a major mistake coming out here or if Sam really even lived in this house or, oh my God, if he'd gotten together with another girl and they were both inside right now.

After a few more agonizing moments, Sam opened the door.

As soon as I saw him, my heart leaped into my throat. I wanted to tumble across the threshold and wrap my arms around his neck. He was barefoot, wearing shorts and a faded blue T-shirt. His hair was longer and his cheeks were scruffier, but otherwise he looked about the same.

As I opened my mouth to speak, he gestured me inside. I followed him up three flights of stairs, into a damp attic, through a window, and onto the roof. We sat next to each other on the loose shingles, watching the sun set over the bay. I could see the arcs of the bridge stretching across the water and the distant hills and lights of San Francisco. I glanced at my toes, where the blisters were finally healing from my night in San Antonio. Then I looked over at his feet, flush against the shingles. I looked at his hands and his shoulders and his face, and I thought about how even if he told me he never wanted to see me again, I'd still be grateful for this time together.

After several minutes Sam turned to me and said, "So."

I tried to remember all the things I'd spent the past seventeen hundred miles preparing to tell him. But before I could say anything, Sam reached over and touched the scar on my forehead. As he did, I thought about how I once believed it all started with the hockey puck. But it really all started when I knocked on the front door of a run-down house in Berkeley, even though I was terrified, even though I knew I could get hurt. And that, in the end, was the true beginning.

ACKNOWLEDGMENTS

I am incredibly grateful to all the people who gave me feedback on this story, helped with child care so I could write, or answered random research questions such as, "What does northern Indiana smell like in early July?" My deepest thanks go out to: Lynn Harris Adelson, Chloe Annetts, Mara Bergman, Judy Blume, Meg Cabot, Anne Dalton, Erin Golden, Jenny Greenberg, Susanna Greenberg, Emma Hofman, Kathleen Jaccarino, Diane Klock, Oliver Kuhn-Wilken, Jeff Layton, Ian Mackler, Miriam Martinez, Megan McCafferty, Jim Miceli, Deborah Noyes Wayshak, Nitsa Papouras-Seidman, Ruth Rath, Stephanie Rath, Jodi Reamer, Amy Reese, Jared and Courtnee Rideout, Neal and Karen Rideout, everyone at Riverside Montessori School, Alison Seidman, Derek Seidman, Michelle Seidman, Chris Smialek, Sonya Sones, Rebecca Wertkin, Debra Wolf, and Anders Wright.

And a special thanks to Jonas and Miles Rideout for filling my life with so much love.